# Titan Encounter

## By Kyle Pratt

William

Thank you for being a part of this. I really look forward to reading your review.

*Kyle Pratt*

July 18, 2013

# Titan Encounter

## Camden Cascade Publishing

Copyright © 2012 Kyle Pratt
ISBN: 0615808948
All Rights Reserved

Cover design and cover art by Micah Hansen

This is a work of fiction. Names, characters, places, especially those on other planets, and incidents either are the product of the author's imagination or are used fictitiously, and any resemblance to actual persons, living or dead, events, or locales is entirely coincidental.

All rights reserved. No part of this book may be used or reproduced in any manner whatsoever without written permission from the author.

## Dedication

Many authors say that their spouse is their biggest fan. My wife Lorraine most certainly is mine. This book would not exist without her constant encouragement and editing.

I would also like to thank my friends and fellow writers, Joyce Scott, Robert Hansen, Barbara Blakey and Carolyn Bickel. You have all taught me so much about the craft of writing.

## Chapter 1

Justin awoke from the nightmare of flashing red lights, whooshing air and voiceless screams only to realize it was not some dark fantasy of his subconscious, it was one of his earliest childhood memories. Every year the calendar forced the images from the black depths of his mind. Slowly he sat up and slid his feet from the edge of the bed to the cold metal floor. His head pounded from too much drink, but his mind would not release the memory.

His mother had shaken him awake on that horrid morning long ago. Even at such a young age, the fear on her face was obvious. Red lights flashed in the compartment. She yanked him from his bed as an explosion rocked the ship. They were under attack. The ship shuddered and with each impact, he cried.

Someone placed him and Mara, in an escape pod and told them to stay. Moments later, he heard a hissing sound and his ears popped. He was only five, but he knew what to do. With all his might, he pushed the hatch shut. Seconds later, his mother appeared in the portal. She banged on the glass and yelled. Together with little Mara, they fought to open the door, pushing the lever and pulling the door, but it wouldn't budge. Tears flowed. The memory of his mother's lifeless face sliding down the portal still haunted him. She was dead because of him.

Sometimes he dreamed that his father was a wealthy merchant from Earth Empire or, if he was a Dreg, that he was a great pirate or smuggler. In either case, Justin imagined that somehow his father would find him and bring him home. It was all just a dream. Mother was dead and Father never came. He stood and his head throbbed in retribution. Stumbling to a portal, he looked at the arid planet far below. *The past is gone.* As he thought the words he meant them but, moments later, his broad shoulders sagged with the memory of the mother he had failed.

He rubbed his aching head then stumbled down the hall. Before he reached Mara's room he knew his sister was gone. Peeking around the half open door, the undisturbed bed confirmed what he already knew. These last few years, when she had the freedom to leave, she had always left him alone on this day. In earlier years, she had tried to console him, but it was a fruitless, wasted effort and she seemed to know it. Clutching his slate in his right hand, he ran fingers across the screen to check his schedule for the day and with a sigh turned to face it.

* * *

Justin watched a vessel inch toward the docking bay one level below, then paused and jotted notes on his slate.

A woman in coveralls approached. Tentatively she asked, "Are you okay?"

He nodded.

"One of the guys said you wanted to talk to me."

Still facing the observation window, he rubbed his pounding head. "Yeah. Mara, could you have someone find these parts and…" He held out the slate, then rubbed his chin with his other hand. "Baxter's aft thermal radiator got shot up on his last run. He'll need a new one." Justin thought for a moment. "Does he pay regularly?" He glanced in her direction.

She nodded.

"Get someone to pull the newest radiator we have from the back so he can see it when he arrives.

"Sure thing."

He turned and for the first time really looked at her stained face and greasy overalls. "What have you been up to?"

"Oh." She grinned under the grime and looked at her clothes and hands. "I helped the night crew install the new decoupler unit in Galt's yacht."

"We hire people to do that, sis."

She pulled a knife from a pocket and began to clean her nails. "Yeah I know."

They discussed the progress of ship repairs in the main bays then Justin asked, "How is the inventory coming?"

"Ah... It's progressing." She wiped her face with a rag, succeeding only in smearing the oil.

Justin wasn't quite sure if he was more annoyed or amused. "We'll discuss it later over dinner." Justin turned and ambled toward his office. "Thanks, Mara."

"Who's cooking?" she called after him.

He smiled, but otherwise ignored her comment. Heading back toward the office, he detected movement off to his right. "What do you need Ferren?"

A man of big proportions waddled into view. His face was covered with a scraggily beard and a bulbous nose. He grinned. "I have something for you."

"You have something for me?" Justin threw his arms to his heart in mock surprise. "Perhaps you have the 20,000 credits you owe me?"

"No..."

"I didn't think so," he said flatly and walked past him.

Ferren followed with effort. His fat torso made him sway when he moved quickly and it was hard for him to talk. With effort, he caught up, then reached out and touched Justin's arm. "But...I salvaged...a ship..."

Not wanting Ferren to have a heart attack, at least not right then, Justin slowed his pace. "We're all business people here Ferren. You're a pirate, not a salvager."

"Okay. We detected a coasting ship, blew a few holes in their hull, and removed the cargo."

Justin smiled. "That's nice. Sell the cargo and pay me."

"When I got back from the run there was word of a man on Bristol paying well for smuggled cargo leaving Earth Empire."

"Yes, I've heard," he said with a growing smile. "So," Justin placed a hand on the pirate's shoulder, "Go to Bristol, sell the cargo, come back and pay me."

"I need fuel cells."

The smile disappeared. "No."

"But remember, I have something for you."

Justin stared at Ferren.

"There was a girl on the ship."

"I don't buy or sell slaves. You know that."

"You can free her."

Justin looked at Ferren with a skeptical eye. "Why would I take her in *partial* payment and then set her free?"

"Maybe you could ransom her?"

"You ransom her and pay me." He turned and walked away.

Huffing and puffing, Ferren chased after him. "I'll make you a very special offer. I'll give you the girl and after selling the cargo I'll pay the 20,000 credits I owe. You keep the girl. Just give me the fuel cells." Every inch of Ferren's face pleaded his case.

"I'm not a slaver."

"After I pay you, free her. You'll have the money and feel good—and maybe you'll be feeling good before I pay you." Ferren thumped Justin's chest.

"I don't like little girls." Justin turned and walked away.

In pursuit Ferren said, "She's not a *little* girl," Ferren said shaking his head, "she's a woman." Once again he was grinning.

"Young, but not too young. About Mara's age, I would guess." His grin grew, showing yellow teeth. "Pretty, like Mara, too."

Justin shuddered at the thought of any woman in the hands of Ferren and his crew. "Leave my sister out of this." Justin stopped, sighed and stared at floor. "Where is this woman from?"

Ferren shrugged. "How would I know?" He stroked his beard. "She's not a Dreg, she has a strange accent."

Justin rubbed his still aching head.

"The ship was coasting at high velocity and was cloaked. I think it was a smuggler."

Justin's eyes widened. "If it was a smuggler, it was probably someone you knew."

A broad grin spread across Ferren's face. "Raiding is what pirates do."

"Sounds like trouble to me."

Ferren waved his hand dismissively, "Smugglers don't complain when they get caught and besides I have friends in high places."

*You have scum for friends.*

"If you don't want her I'll sell her for what I can, but I'm willing to *give* her to you, my friend."

*We're not friends.* Memories of his own arrival in this armpit of a system surged into his mind. The smell of the slave market was nauseating, but that was easy to cope with. Mara's tears had been the hardest to deal with. The images still tore at him. He pushed hard against the memories, forcing them back into the dark depths. "28,000."

"What?"

"If I agree," he wagged his finger for emphasis, "you give me the girl and, immediately after you sell the cargo, I get the 20,000 credits you already owe me and 8,000 for the fuel cells."

"They're not worth 8,000!"

"Well, get them from Rumon. Oh…" Justin paused and looked serious, "don't you owe him even more than you owe me?" He rubbed his chin. "Hmmm, what about Rasnic? No. No, didn't he threaten to kill you?"

Ferren stared into his eyes. "You're a hard man."

Justin shrugged. "I sell junk parts to pirates. What do you expect?"

"I'll bring in the girl."

## Chapter 2

The light flickered casting the room in alternating shadow and light. Looking up from his sketch pad, Justin's wondered if it would remain on or would the tiny room be cast into darkness. For now the light held.

Sitting in the corner he looked at the nearby wall. *Gray. My world exists in shades of gray.* Childhood memories of a green world with blue rivers and sky still haunted his mind, but they were recollections, or dreams. He sighed and the desire to breath fresh air, not the stale brew of the old microworld, weighed upon his mind. *I need a vacation.* His tongue slid across his lips. *And a drink.*

A drop of water ran down a line of rust on the bulkhead beside him. *Okay, it's not all gray.* He chuckled that a corroded pipe provided a rare display of color. *Perhaps I could paint a mural in this compartment.* He shook his head. *No.* It was just a utility room. He casually scraped the rust with his fingernail, then returned his attention to a sketch of a tree-lined valley with a river winding through it. Around him were half a dozen drawings of trees and flowers. Some were fanciful, others realistic, but all were colorful.

He looked at the young woman lying on a cot against the far wall. Her mouth hung slightly open exposing perfect ivory white teeth. Physically she was about the same height, weight and build as his sister. Both were lean and statuesque, reminiscent of an athlete, but the woman before him had more muscle. Both shared the auburn hair that he found attractive and both women kept their hair longer than the current style. Mara did so to cover the implant at the back of her head. He had checked just after Ferren and his thugs had left, the woman on the bunk had no implant. Ferren was right this mystery woman was pretty. Her hair flowed past the pillow and over the side of the cot like water cascading over falls.

Hanging from her neck was a gold medallion on a simple chain. Hidden under her clothing when brought in, it had fallen out as the men plopped her on the cot. Ferren had attempted to take the object. "Take the value off of your bill," Justin insisted.

His eyes drifted from the medal. For several moments he watched as her breasts rose and fell with each breath. Any man would consider her worth the antique fuel cells he had given Ferren. He stood to get a better view of her face, then flipped the page of the drawing pad and started sketching her as she was, sleeping with hair pouring to one side, but he added just a hint of a smile. He looked back at his sleeping subject. *If Ferren never pays me, I'll still be glad I saved you from him and the market.* He stepped closer. His eyes focused on her full lips as he sketched the sleeping angel. *She isn't just pretty, she is beautiful.*

She moaned slightly. The drug was wearing off. Hours earlier when Ferren and his men had carried her in, he had asked why she was unconscious.

"She was in a stasis chamber in the cargo bay." Ferren gave a wicked grin. "Probably a present for somebody."

She coughed.

His hand froze in mid stroke. He held his breath. His gaze rested easily upon her eyes.

Her lashes fluttered.

Justin glanced at his sketch and closed the pad.

Her head turned. Her eyes opened.

He smiled. "Hello,"

Eyes wide, her mouth opened, but no sound came forth.

He shook his head. "You're safe."

The young woman tried to stand, but fell with her back against the wall. "Who are you?"

"Justin. My name is Justin."

Her eyes darted right and left. "Where am I? What did you do with him?"

"Who?"

Like a leopard she leaped to the corner and grabbed a length of pipe in her left hand. "The man I was traveling with—my father…" Holding the weapon like a bat she demanded, "Did you kill him?"

## Chapter 3

"Calm down," Justin said, while holding his hands low and apart.

She took a deep breath.

Slowly he stepped forward.

"Don't come any closer." She raised the pipe. "I'll hit you." She looked about the small room. "Where is he? What have you done with him?"

"You were the only one they brought to me."

She swung.

He ducked.

Momentum carried her partly around. Justin lunged for her side and with a thud they hit the deck.

"You're quick," he said pinning her arms down.

"Release me!" She shouted as she struggled to free the hand the held the pipe. "What did you do with him?" She demanded. Then before he could answer, she cursed him. "Did you kill him?"

Still holding her arms to the floor he shook his head. "No. I mean…I haven't killed anyone." *Well, lately anyway.*

"Is he alive?" Her eyes pleaded.

"I don't know.

"What *do* you know, pirate?" Contempt flowed with the words.

Justin marveled that even pinned to the floor she was defiant. "I'm not a pirate," he said defensively. *I sell things to pirates, I repair their ships, but I'm not one.*

"Then why are you holding me captive?"

"I'm not."

She turned and looked at her arms, still firmly held to the ground, on either side of her head.

"Okay. Okay. I'll make you a deal—let go of the pipe and promise not to hit me with anything and I'll let go."

She pushed with both arms and flung a knee toward his groin.

Both attempts failed. Justin sat on her stomach and for a moment stared into her defiant eyes. "Let the pipe go."

The icy stare slowly melted into acquiescence. "I accept your proposal." The pipe rolled a few millimeters from her hand.

Cautiously he released her and stood.

In one smooth motion she jumped to her feet in a crouched defensive stance.

Justin stepped back unsure of what would happen next.

Slowly she uncoiled into an erect, but tense, posture. "How did I come to be here and," she looked about, "where am I?"

"You're on the microworld Liberty, in the Confederation of Free States."

"The warlord territories." A slight drop of the jaw registered her surprise at the news. "You're a Dreg."

"Yes," he nodded, "but we prefer the term citizen and CFS." He breathed deeply. "As to how you got here, well, your ship was raided by pirates two days ago…"

She slowly nodded as if remembering the events.

"...and this morning you were given to me in partial payment for a debt."

"Given to you?" Cold eyes bored through him. "I am a citizen of Earth Empire."

Justin shrugged. "Well, the CFS doesn't recognize the government of Earth Empire, or its laws."

The woman stepped back. "Am I your slave?"

Over the six years he had run the business he had received half-a-dozen people as payment. It had been easy to set them free, but looking at the beautiful woman that stood before him he was sorely tempted to exercise his legal rights, but Mara and his own conscience would not let him. He took a deep breath and sighed. "No." He shook his head. *I may deal with scum, but I'm not one of them.* "You're free to go, but I don't recommend it."

"And why not?"

"Do you have any money or valuables?"

She clutched the medallion that hung from her neck, stuffed it in her shirt and shook her head. "I'm sure the pirates have it all."

"Do you know how to contact your family?"

The question seemed to shake her to the core. "If my father is dead, then I have no family."

Her despair seemed to flow into him. "I'm sorry to hear that. You are free to stay here until you can arrange something but..." the desires that welled up within him made his next words hard to say but, he felt, all the more important to declare, "you *are* free."

She seemed to look at him for the first time as a person, not a scoundrel. "My name is Naomi. What did you say your name was?"

He relaxed just a little. "Justin."

"Tell me Justin, why do you accept people in payment and then set them free?"

"Because I've been in your position."

\*   \*   \*

Five days later Justin sat at his desk going over accounts receivable. He lifted his eyes and stared at the closed door of his office. Maybe it was a faint sound or fleeting shadow, but he knew someone was coming. Then with a certainty he had come to trust, and hide, he knew who was coming. In a moment, the door to his office would open. *What do you want now Ferren?*

The pirate sauntered in.

*I need a secretary.*

"Mara said you were here."

*Thanks Sis.* Years ago DNA tests proved that he and Mara were not related but, as he looked at the pirate's piss-colored teeth, he was glad Mara had agreed with him and not revealed the results. Ferren waddled forward in a gaudy, new suit.

His eyes lingered on the door. "I've watched your sister grow into a remarkable and handsome woman."

*My customers are the scum of the CFS.* Then a smile crossed Justin's face. *Naomi might make a good secretary.* He stood. "Is there something I can help you with?"

Ferren spread his arms wide and smiled, "I've come to pay you!"

"You didn't have to come here to pay me." He sat back down. *And from now on don't.*

"I wanted to make sure you got your money, and I have other business to discuss."

Justin sighed as he thought that payment might not be forthcoming. "What other business?"

"First things, first," Ferren said enthusiastically, "Let me pay what I owe you." He pulled out his slate.

Justin eyed the pirate. *You're going to pay me? On time?* "Well, in a way, I'm glad you're here." He sat down. "I have something I want to discuss with you."

"Oh?" he said as he pressed his thumb on the screen and sat. The seat seemed to groan under his ponderous posterior.

"You said Naomi was in stasis when you found her, but…"

"Who?"

"The girl you gave me last week, her name is Naomi."

"Yes. She was in stasis."

"But she knew the ship had been attacked." Justin could almost hear the pirate's heart pound in his chest. "She tells me she fought your men."

"She did! She fought like a tigress. We darted her." He smiled. "Didn't want to damage the goods."

"Did you take anyone else captive from that ship?"

"Why so many questions?"

"Just curious." Justin smiled politely. "That was the last question, I promise."

"The crew wanted to fight. We killed them."

"This would have been an older man, not a member of the crew."

Ferren looked concerned. "Has she gotten to you? She's nobody. Let me take her off your hands."

Justin waved his hand. "About the older man.."

"We killed him," the pirate said matter-of-factly as he punched numbers in his slate.

"Why?"

He looked up. "Why not?" He paused for a moment as if he expected a reply, but none came so he returned to the slate. "He was of no value and besides he shot at us and blocked our way to the cargo bay."

"He was the girl's father."

Ferren looked up and grinned, exposing the rot that passed as his mouth. "I'll pay you for anything she has cost you." He leaned forward and chuckled. "What do you want for her?"

Leaning back to avoid the pirate's bad breath Justin said, "She's not for sale." Justin fumbled with his slate. "Have you transferred the funds?"

"Tell me how much more to add for the girl."

Justin shook his head.

"Everyone has their price."

"I already set her free."

Concern spread across Ferren's face. "Have you registered the emancipation?"

"I will." Justin felt a wave of desperation from the pirate.

The fat man's face turned cold, but his eyes were like hot daggers.

The hair on the back of Justin's neck stood. He eased his hand toward a gun installed years before under the desk.

Ferren's words came slowly. "We'll discuss her later." He breathed deeply and slid the slate into his pocket. "You've been paid in full." Just a hint of a grin crossed his face, "Now about your sister."

"What about her?"

The fat man stood and spoke with a sincere tone of voice. "I have a good ship, the Acheron, and a good crew. Thanks to this last job I have no debts." He paused and squared his shoulders. "It is time for me to marry, and I have chosen your sister."

Justin's eyes widened in disbelief. "No."

"Why not?"

"I don't have to give a reason."

Again, Ferren's face turned cold. Justin's fingers inched toward the gun.

"You've come far, from slave to freeman, but…well, what family do you have? Who is your family?"

*I wish I knew.* "Are you done?"

"No." Ferren achieved a thoughtful look. 'You manage your business well and you're a good salesman and a successful entrepreneur and now you think you're better than the rest of us…"

*Yes—I am.* "No, I don't."

"…however my family is one of the oldest in the Confederation of Free States. A powerful family…"

I know. I pay protection money to your uncle every month.

"descended from two senators from the last free government of Earth; my family is still powerful in the CFS."

*Your cousin bought a seat in the senate.*

Ferren bent forward. "And my new friend from the Empire just bought all the cargo from my last run, and he wants the Earth girl."

"Naomi?" *She's from Earth?*

Ferren nodded. "He paid well for the cargo, but he wanted everything from the ship, cargo, survivors and even the bodies. He's willing to pay well for the girl."

"Why bodies and survivors?"

"Why should I care?" Ferren raised his arms in exasperation. "We can both profit from this. He pays well for the Earth girl, we share that money, and I pay well for Mara." He stood as tall and straight. "Name your price for both of them, I can pay it."

"No sale." *You fat pig.* Justin's finger rested on the trigger.

Their eyes locked for several moments.

"I'll have them both." The pirate turned and slowly walked away.

## Chapter 4

Justin's words came slowly and gently, to soften the blow of the message, "So, Ferren said that you were the only survivor on the ship. Your father didn't...."

Tears welled in Naomi's eyes. "I hope that someday I have the opportunity to kill that pirate."

"I've wished the same thing once or twice, but he has nasty friends. I don't recommend it."

A few seconds later, she walked to the window overlooking the main docking bay. Justin joined her and together for several moments they stood at the window overlooking the bustling cargo bay below.

"These people, they all work for you." It was more of a statement, than a question.

He nodded.

"You are prosperous?"

He smiled. "Yes."

"But you live off the death and destruction of others."

"What?" The statement felt like a blow.

"You seem a better, nobler sort than this."

"Thank you—I think."

As a tear rolled down her cheek, she nodded. "Yes. You are like a king who lives in a sewer. You may be a king, but your subjects are only the vermin of the dark." She turned, wiped her face and walked from the office.

Seconds later Mara entered. "Naomi's crying." Her eyes narrowed. "What did you do?"

Justin, still pondering Naomi's words, frowned. "It wasn't me, well maybe…sort of." He reiterated the information Ferren had provided.

Mara looked back at the door. "I guess we both know how she feels." She stood beside Justin for a moment looking down at the bay below. "I feel awful."

"Why?"

"Because when I saw her crying, I was coming here to ask how long she would be staying."

Justin frowned and shook his head.

"I didn't know you had just told her she was an orphan." Her mouth agape, words seemed to stumble forth. "And…and I said I felt bad about it. I…I was just," she shrugged, "wondering."

Together they stared out the window for several seconds.

"So, ah…just for planning purposes—how long will Naomi be staying with us?"

"You're cold, Mara." Justin turned to her. "Do you want me to kick her out today?"

"No, not today." She sighed. "You've got me flustered, that wasn't how I meant it."

Justin stared at her. "So, it's my fault you're upset?"

"Yeah, sort of…."

"She's a good worker and," turning back to the window, he continued, "she's been doing a bright job on the inventory you procrastinated on."

"I've always been better with the mechanical work than the administrative stuff." A hand whipped around, brushing her long hair aside and exposing the implant at the base of her skull. "That's why Garrett had this put in the back of my head."

Justin's gut tightened. He hated to recall the day Garrett, their former master, had Mara implanted and he was sure she knew that.

She sighed and her eyes softened "and besides I don't think she has been open with us."

"What's that supposed to mean?"

She ran her fingers through her hair. "I've always marveled at your ability to tell if someone was trying to deceive you…."

"What's your point?"

"I think your genitals are blocking the path to your brain."

Justin rolled his eyes

"What do we know about her?"

He frowned as his eyes narrowed. "We know enough—she's a good worker."

"And I'm not?"

*There's no way I'm going to win this argument.* "This is not about you." He picked up his slate from the desk and marched from the office. *My genitals blocking the path to my brain!* He turned down the passageway. *I'm an intelligent grown man—a good businessman, not some hormone-driven adolescent. Sure Naomi is attractive.* He took a left and strode down another passageway. "But that hasn't affected my judgment. *Mara is jealous, that's all—jealous.* He headed down a flight of stairs. *We know enough about her. We know….* He stopped midway down the stairs as he recalled what he did know about Naomi. *She is a good worker. Her father traveled on business and she had accompanied him.* He also knew that Naomi was from Earth, but that information had come from Ferren. *And why is someone so willing to pay the pirate for the cargo, bodies, and survivors of the ship?*

Justin sighed deeply. *I need a drink.* He had disagreed with Mara in the past, they had yelled and cursed each other on occasion, but he had come to respect her opinion. *Okay, Mara, you're right, we really don't know much about Naomi.*

He continued downstairs to the main level. Just ahead was a woman barely out of her teens. Maybe six years younger than Justin, he had hired her as an apprentice welder. "Congratulations on the baby."

She smiled, "Thanks." Then her face turned dark. "Did Roark tell you? I told him not to say anything yet. I'm so going to…"

"No, he didn't tell me."

She put her hands on her belly and looked down. "I'm not showing already am I?"

Moving away as fast as he could he said, "No, you look fine."

"Then how did you know?"

He rounded the corner and nearly ran for the airlock into the main cargo bay. *How did I know she was pregnant?* Entering the bay, the sight of Naomi pushed all concerns from his mind. Approaching the corner where she sat, staring at a blank wall, he coughed.

She jumped. "Oh, you startled me." Her eyes were red and puffy.

"I'm sorry," he bit his lip, "about everything. Ah…well, I'd like you to come to dinner at our quarters this evening."

She looked up in the direction of the private quarters. "Dinner? With you?"

Justin nodded. "Yes, and my sister?" *I hope you don't mind Mara.*

"Really, I am okay. There is no need…."

"It's not just about the bad news. I want to get to know my new employee."

Naomi's eyes widened. "There is not much to know about me."

Her nervousness at the idea of dinner emboldened him. "Then we'll have more time to enjoy the food."

"Ah…you are kind, but…."

"I insist." Justin smiled, turned, and walked away.

\*   \*   \*

Hands planted on her hips, Mara said, "You want me to cook dinner for your date?"

"It's not a date. You're going to be here and you said we didn't know much about her."

"Then ask her questions. Use a little alcohol, but not my cooking."

"Please Sis. You're a brighter cook than I'll ever be."

"Get a wife."

*I'm working on it.* "Speaking of wives, earlier today Ferren made an offer to marry you."

Mara shuddered. "What did you say?"

*Oh, this could be fun.* Forcing a blank expression on his face, he glanced at her. "You know Ferren is from an old and powerful family. Networking with his family and friends would help my business."

Mara stared at him.

Justin avoided her gaze. "He came into some money recently and has paid off his debts."

He could feel her eyes bore into him. "He's got a good ship."

He turned.

Their eyes locked.

He smiled.

She grinned back at him. "You never could lie to me."

"I told him 'no,' but he did ask."

She pulled a knife from her trousers and gave it a little flick. "The day you say "Yes," will be the last day Ferren is fertile."

They both laughed

She sighed. "All right, you clean, I'll cook."

"Thank you." Still grinning he asked, "Do you always carry a knife?"

Coyly she raised an eyebrow. "Some things a girl needs to keep secret."

The smell of the food wafted over the apartment as Justin finished setting the table. He called over his shoulder, "Come on Mara, she'll be here any minute."

The door to Mara's bedroom opened and she leaned against the doorframe wearing a pastel blue dress that draped from one shoulder. "How do I look?" Pearls dangled from her ears and graced her neck.

He turned and looked her up and down. "You shine up pretty bright, Sis." *I wonder where the knife is.* Images of Naomi in the dress and pearls floated through his mind. He smiled.

Mara smiled back. "Well, I want to look good for you and," she said flatly, "your date."

"It's not a date."

She shrugged as the housesys announced their visitor. A holo image appeared of Naomi wearing the same green coveralls she had worn for days.

Justin opened the door with a broad smile.

Golden tan-colored walls greeted Naomi as she entered their home. Her eyes slowly swept the room. "The quarters I've seen here have all been cramped and gray, but this is a nice size for two and the mix of colors is very warm and pleasant."

"That's my brother. He's always had a bright eye for color and design."

For several minutes, they talked and walked, slowly about the living room. Naomi stopped in front of each sketch or painting that hung on the wall. Most were of valleys, rivers, mountains, and brooks.

"Who is this?" she asked, looking at a picture of an older man with gray hair and beard in a green military style uniform.

"It may be someone from my past." He shrugged. "I don't really know. I painted it from several vague memories and a bit of imagination."

Naomi smiled and started to move on, but Mara stepped forward. The two almost collided. Mara's gaze locked on the picture. "Look at the medallion around his neck."

"So?" Justin asked.

Mara pointed to the picture, then to the medal around Naomi's neck.

Justin's eyes narrowed as he looked between the two. The medallion that hung from the collar of the man was similar to the one that hung around the neck of Naomi. Both were gold and etched with two intersecting arcs. The ends of the lines on the right side extended beyond the meeting point and created the simple outline of a fish in profile.

Both Mara and Justin stared at her and the object that hung from her neck.

Naomi clutched the medal. "It was my father's. He gave it to me." She stepped back and released it between her breasts. "I did not steal it."

"No," Justin said, waving a hand. "I didn't think you did. I don't even know who this man is."

"Strange coincidence, that's for sure," Mara added.

He nodded. "Do you know anything about it?"

She shook her head. "It is just a trinket." Stepping back again, she turned to the table. "The food looks lovely."

"Yes." Justin's thoughts still lingered on the medallion, but he tried to smile politely. "You should recognize several of the items. These," he said pointing to a dish of mixed vegetables," are terraform varieties from Earth

"I recognize peas and corn, but I'm not from Earth."

Justin's eyebrow rose slightly. "Oh?"

"No, Epsilon. My family is from Epsilon," she said as they sat around the table.

\* \* \*

"That was the best meal I've had in many days," Naomi said, looking at Justin. "Did you cook it?"

"No," he started clearing the table, "Mara is the brighter cook."

As Justin returned with a strawberry cake for dessert, Mara asked the first substantive question of the evening, "Why were you traveling outside of the Empire?"

"My father was on his way to Gatewai. I just went along."

"Really?" Justin's eyes widened in surprise, "Your father was going out beyond the CFS?"

She nodded.

"Does that ancient jump-gate work?" Justin asked as he sat.

Mara shook her head. "No, I don't think so..."

Turning to Naomi Justin asked, "But someone is expecting you there?"

"They were expecting my father." She squirmed a bit in her seat. "But I don't know who they were."

Mara swallowed a bite of cake then asked. "What kind of business was your father in?"

"Terraforming." She smiled. "He was a freelance engineer."

"You must have been very proud of him."

"I thought they had given up terraforming that system." He turned to Naomi. "Your father…what did you say his name was?"

"Ah, Saul, Dr. Carl Saul."

"Oh?" He rubbed his chin.

"Have you heard of him?" Mara asked.

Justin shook his head slowly. "No."

"It was a small consulting business," Naomi added.

Justin stood and collected the plates from the table, balancing them on his arm like a waiter. Still leaning over the table he said, "Your father must have business associates back in the empire, have you been able to contact any of them?"

Her eyes slid down. "Not yet."

Mara frowned. "I'm sure you will soon, but you're welcome to stay here as long…"

Naomi shook her head. "As soon as I have the money and can make the arrangements I would like to leave." She bit her lip. "That did not come out right." Her eyes darted between them. "You have both been very kind, but I really cannot stay here."

"Of course," Mara said. "We understand, but until you can return home, do let us know if you need anything. I'm sure Justin or I can help."

Naomi fumbled with her fork. "Thank you for the meal, but it is late. I should go."

Mara stood, "Come on." Reaching out, she took her arm. "I'll walk with you back to your quarters." As they walked toward the door she looked Naomi up and down. "You're about my size and build. Could you use some clothes?"

Naomi chuckled. "Well maybe something to wear when I recycle this."

As they left, Justin walked to the counter and poured himself a drink. With a quick tilt of the head, he poured the golden brew down. The hair on the back of Justin's neck still bristled, and that feeling, that old feeling in the pit of his stomach, lingered. He poured himself another drink then shook his head. He didn't want to believe it, but he knew it was so. Naomi's whole story had been a lie.

## Chapter 5

Justin bolted upright in bed. His eyes darted to every corner of the room, but he heard no sound or movement. With one hand he wiped cold sweat and drool from his face. Dim light came in through the window overlooking the main passageway, but otherwise the room was dark. *What woke me?* He looked at his clock beside the bed. The power was out.

*Help!*

Mara's voice shouted inside his head. For a moment he thought it was his imagination, but it came again as if she were inside his brain. He jumped from bed, grabbed a gun and his pants, and ran down the hall to her room. It was empty, the bed unused. *Where are you?* Then he knew. Somehow, he knew. Justin turned and headed for the cargo bay. Gun in hand, he stumbled down the stairs while pulling on his pants. *Don't shoot your foot!*

The pale glow of backup lights met him as he emerged from the stairwell on the main level. The air lock to the first cargo bay was open. Using two hands he snapped his gun to the ready position as he stepped into the tiny compartment and heard Naomi scream in pain.

He hunched low, moved into the bay, and darted swiftly behind a tool caddie. He scanned the room. The women were outnumbered, but they didn't appear to need much help. Mara's knife protruded from the chest of a man on the deck before him. A few meters away Mara, still in her dress, had her hands tight around the throat of a man. Someone grabbed her from behind.

Mara head-butted him then kneed the man before her in the groin.

Both men stumbled.

Mara hit the one before her as Justin shot the one behind.

On the far side of the bay, Naomi pounced on the throat of one man, performed a perfect pirouette, and shattered the jaw of another. His blood painted the bulkhead beside him. She grabbed a metal bar and used it to catapult herself onto her next victim. Remembering their first meeting in the utility room, he smiled. *The woman sure likes metal pipes.*

Mara was street brawling while Naomi performed a dance of destruction. Justin smiled, then saw Ferren moving toward Naomi. He fired his weapon, just missing the pirate's head. He cursed as the fat blob ducked behind a crate.

The women were mopping up the last of the other men.

Rage consumed Justin. He marched across the bay firing his gun. He cursed the pirate. *You're the cause of this!*

\*     \*     \*

"Justin," Mara shouted from across the bay, then in a softer tone, as if to gently awaken someone, she repeated herself. "Justin."

Justin's eyes followed his outstretched arm as it reached into the air. His hand seemed to hold something, but it was empty. Only then did he realize that Ferren hung in the air, two meters above his empty grasp. The bloated bag of bilge turned a pastel shade of blue as his fingers frantically clawed and scratched at the invisible hand that held him high by the throat. Justin looked from the pirate to Mara. "How?"

Ferren fell to the ground and gasped.

Two meters away, a look of astonishment spread across Mara's face.

Naomi's eyes grew wide with fear. "Are you a Nephilim?" She backed away.

Ferren again gulped air, then shouted, "Titan," and stumbled backward.

Naomi and Ferren ran in opposite directions. Mara chased after Ferren, but the fat pirate like a cockroach motivated by terror and self-preservation, darted through a hatch and slammed it shut.

Crashing into it, Mara cursed. When she managed to open it he was gone. She cursed again and locked it.

"Naomi, help me shut and locked the hatches."

Justin looked over the bay. Ten dead, and dying, men littered the deck. "She's gone," he said then melted to the floor.

Mara ran for the nearest hatch.

Justin, his strength spent, knew he should get up, but instead, continued to lay face up, gazing at an emergency light while replaying the battle in his mind. *How did I hold Ferren in the air?* He shook his head. No logical answer came to him. *How did the girls kill ten, armed men?* Naomi was clearly a trained fighter, but they could have shot her. *They wanted her alive. No! Ferren wanted both of the women alive, Naomi for the mysterious buyer from Earth and Mara for himself.*

Still his mind was troubled: Ten men should be more than capable of handling two women, even if one was a well-trained fighter and the other a good brawler.

Slowly he sat up and began reloading his gun while still pondering the fight. The regular lights came on Mara entered the docking bay. Standing a few meters from Justin she haltingly asked, "Are you all right?"

Still sitting on the floor, he breathed heavily then placed the gun on the deck. For the first time he noticed her dress was torn and bloodstained. He clutched the damp material. "Is this your blood?"

"No. Come on, we should leave here."

He tried to stand. "However I did that," he held up his arm as he did when Ferren floated above him, "it drained me. I can't focus. My arms are like lead weights." His arm dropped to the ground. "All I want to do is rest, but I think I'm okay—or will be." He looked at the spot where Ferren had dropped to the deck. "How did I do that?"

"I don't know, but we'll deal with it together."

"Naomi thinks I'm one of the Nephilim."

She smiled. "They're a myth."

"Am I a Titan?"

"You're not a cloned killer."

"Killer?" he mumbled. Memories of Garrett, their former owner, flashed through his mind.

"Yeah," she looked at him strangely. "You know, supposedly the Titans had god-like powers they used to kill their enemies."

*I am a killer.* "Killing someone…isn't that what I was doing?" Justin rubbed his throbbing head.

"Remember all those history books you made me read while we were growing up?"

Justin grinned. "I read them, too."

"Well, according to those books, the Nephilim led the humans to victory over the Titans during The Titanomachy War." She waved her hand dismissively. "The Titans were all killed."

He looked about searching for something. "So, what am I? What other choices are there?"

"I don't know, but right now we have a bigger problem."

He frowned, "What?"

She looked around a bay strewn with bodies and blood. "Ferren will report this to the authorities."

He nodded. "Ferren's alive and no one will care that these thugs were killed."

"But they will care about what you did, that mental power you apparently have, and since I'm pretty sure you're not Nephilim, they'll burn you at the stake in front of the Hall of Justice as a Titan."

## Chapter 6

There hadn't been such an execution in Justin's lifetime, but he had seen the historical vids from centuries past and the laws were still on the books. He came up on one knee. Mara helped him to his feet.

Reluctantly the realization formed. Moments ago, using some sort of psychic ability, he had held Ferren in the air and just yesterday he had known that Ferren stood outside his office. Later, he had known the young woman in the hall was pregnant, and that night he knew Naomi lied during the dinner.

Justin feared what the authorities might find if they performed a detailed analysis of his DNA. He didn't believe the stories from the Empire about the Nephilim, god-like spirit warriors guiding and assisting mortals, and didn't for a moment believe he could be one. That left one option. The Titan soldiers had used their psychic abilities to slaughter millions but, unlike the Nephilim, the Titans claimed to be human. *My parents may have been Titans.*

"I'm not channeling some ancient warrior god." He shuddered and turned toward Mara. "I've got to hide…" He froze for a moment then added softly, "Somewhere." He stepped forward, gave her a hug, then kissed her forehead. "Goodbye."

"Oh, no." She shook her head and stepped back, but held his hands tight "We may not be brother and sister, but…well…my earliest memory is in that escape pod with you and seeing your mother…." Her voice trailed off, her eyes fell to the floor. "I've always felt that wherever we were from, our families had been close." She paused and when she spoke again her voice was a whisper. "You've cared for me and," she looked up, tears welling in her eyes, "I've always cared for you." Jaw set and eyes intense she declared, "Where you go, I go."

"In minutes I'm going to be a wanted man." He was closer to tears than he wanted her to know. "I don't know where I'm going. I…."

"I'm going with you."

He knew it wasn't smart for her to come. He knew he should forbid it. But she had always been there, his sister in every way but blood. He could not imagine living without her. At some level it shamed him, but if life was going to get tough, he wanted her by his side. He squeezed her hand. "Okay." Turning he looked at the ship in the bay. "This is just a sublight hopper. What's the fastest FTL ship we have?"

"Galt's yacht, the Surfeit, in bay Three. We just finished the refit."

The ship specifications ran through his mind: medium range FTL drive; back up fission reactor; small auxiliary skiff. "Great. Get everything you'll need and meet me there in five minutes."

Minutes later Justin came down the passageway toward the yacht with two duffle bags full of clothing, food, guns, and ammo. Under one arm he carried sketch books. Too weary to lift the bags he dragged them.

Naomi stepped from a side passage three meters ahead with a gun pointed at his chest. "Only a Nephilim or Titan could do what you did. Which are you?"

Fear and determination flowed from her like waves into Justin's consciousness. He looked her in the eye. "I'm not Nephilim."

The gun remained pointed at his chest. "I believe you. I've never seen a Nephilim show mercy or kindness, but," she pressed the targeting button and a red dot appeared on Justin's chest, "neither did the Titans."

"All the Titans were killed," he said.

"How can you be certain?"

Frustration brewed within him. "Look, I don't have time for a debate right now."

She ignored him. "The Nephilim still fear the Titans."

Justin sensed that she was telling the truth and wondered how she would know what the Nephilim feared. He tugged the bags. "I really need to be leaving."

Her aim remained fixed on his chest.

Tentatively he stepped forward. "I don't know what I am."

She bit her lip and seemed to mull his answer. "Are you some new kind of messenger or prophet?"

"Okay. Great. I'm some kind of new Nephilim. A prophet. Lower the gun."

"You are being sarcastic." Naomi stared at him intently. "If you are deity then, forgive me Lord." She took a step forward, stared intently at him, then squinted. A dagger seemed to stab from inside his skull. The sketchpads slipped from under his arm.

Memories flew through his mind like a torrent, but backwards from the present. Suddenly he was strangling Ferren. Then he was imagining Naomi in Mara's blue dress mere hours before. In a flash, he was staring down at Naomi as she lay unconscious with her hair flowing over the side of the cot that first day. The desires of that moment stirred again. Then he was bargaining with Ferren, and Naomi was part of the price. Those events faded as earlier events flowed to life. He was negotiating to free a family, even earlier giving the father a job. Next, he was freeing the man moments after he had been given in payment. In flashes he saw himself doing the mundane tasks of life, but also giving money and assistance to others. But he also saw Garrett, who had treated him like a son. The man he had murdered.

Days of floating in an escape pod with Mara flowed backward through his mind until the moment of his mother's death rushed into his consciousness. He saw her as if for the first time dying on the wrong side of the portal. Mara cried beside him. He shook his head violently. "No!" The sketchpads hit the ground. Pages floated in the air and spilled across the deck.

The gun flew from Naomi's hand and crumpled like a toy in midair. She stumbled backward, barely maintaining her footing.

"I've got to go. Out of my way." He flung his hand to the side as if to sweep her away.

Naomi flew against the wall.

He felt her struggle. Somehow his mind held her to the bulkhead.

They glanced at the crushed weapon at her feet. Frantically she resisted his mental grasp.

Weariness gave way to exhaustion. "Stop. Stop. Whatever I am, I won't hurt you." His tired arm collapsed to his side.

She collapsed to her knees. "You are a Titan?" It was both a statement and a question.

*No. Don't think so, but how then did I disarm you, hold you against the bulkhead and nearly strangle Ferren?* "I didn't mean to scare you." He stared at Naomi's pleading eyes. He sat on one duffle bag with his head in hands. *What am I?*

"It is indeed confusing. You have powers only the Nephilim or Titans possess…

*Did I ask that out loud?*

"…but you show mercy and kindness."

*Mercy? Kindness?*

"You set me free and have treated me with kindness. I had a gun pointed at you, but you did not kill me when you could have."

A myriad of thoughts bubbled in the back of his mind. *Am I crazy? How many god-like beings does Naomi know, or think she knows? Is she crazy?* But one idea pushed to the front of his mind. *Can she hear my thoughts?*

*Yes, if you wish it.*

*No!* He shook his head, then grabbed it with both hand. *No!*

He felt her mind shut to him like a door slamming closed.

*I'm crazy.* Justin stood. *I'm hearing voices.* "I need to get to the cargo bay." The duffle bags hardly moved under the pull of his tired arms.

Standing, she said, "I must flee this place also. Please allow me to accompany you."

"Why would you want to come with us?"

Frantic words poured forth. "I am sure Ferren will attempt to kidnap me again. It is best that I leave before his next attempt." She looked about. "If you and Mara are gone, there is no one to hold me to this place. You and Mara are the only friends I have."

It was true, there was nothing for her here. She would surely be snatched and sold to Ferren's mystery buyer. Even without that threat, her youth, beauty, and innocence would lead to her quick victimization. He looked into her eyes and knew that he did not want to leave her behind. "Perhaps we can find a safe place for you. Come on," he said and moved slowly forward with bags in tow.

She nodded as he passed. "Do you need help with that?"

Exhausted from the fights, Justin offered her the lighter of the two bags.

He dragged his bag into the bay. Mara had arrived first and, still in her torn and blood stained dress, wrestled with docking cables.

Pulling hard on a cable tie down, she turned and smiled, "You found Naomi!" Looking at the other woman she asked, "Have you decided he's not a demigod?"

"No."

Justin frowned at Naomi then shrugged as he turned back to Mara.

She yanked the cable with renewed vigor and it fell to the ground.

"What is that?" Naomi tilted her head up with her eyes half closed.

Justin and Mara stopped. Only the sound of the air handler was audible at first. Then came the distant wail of an alarm and muffled shouts.

"Naomi, get those bags on the Ship. Mara, spin up the engines. We've got to leave."

"Where are we going?"

I have no idea.

## Chapter 7

Justin grabbed a long-handled wrench and ran back down the passageway where he had met Naomi moments before. At the far end he slammed the hatch closed, locked it, and then jammed the door with the tool. It wouldn't stop whoever was coming, but it would slow them down.

He dashed back up a flight of stairs, and into the control room. Quickly he surveyed the bays below. Police were already in the first one looking at the bodies. Glancing to his right he noted the glow from the ship engines in bay three. Mara would soon be ready to launch. His fingers flashed over the controls as he entered the code to open the external doors.

Alarms sounded.

Red lights flashed.

The police looked up and fired at Justin.

Glass shattered.

He dropped to his knees.

A computer voice advised, "Warning! The external doors of bay three will open in 30 seconds." Pumps sucked air from the dock.

Still crouching, a thought came to him and he entered the codes to open the other external doors. He smiled. *That'll keep them busy for a while.*

Red lights flashed as the computer repeated the warning for the other docking bays, Justin ran from the room. Grabbing the railings at the top of the stairs, he flew down them hardly touching a step. The entrance to bay three had automatically sealed, but he entered via the airlock. As he dashed across the hold he gasped for air and his ears popped painfully. Running up the ramp, he stumbled, then lunged into the open airlock of the ship.

\*     \*     \*

Justin's head throbbed with each beat of his heart. He pushed the nightmare of red lights and suffocation from his mind and forced open his eyes only to wince in pain as subdued light hit his pupils. It was several minutes before he tried again to gradually open them. Even the dim light was painful, and he had trouble focusing the image. He lay on a bed in an unfamiliar compartment. The walls were an ivory white, the furnishings simple but stylish. The blanket over him was woven in shades of blue. He sighed. *I'm not in jail.* He tried to stand, but nausea swept over him and he collapsed back on the bed. *I'll stay here for a while.*

Several minutes passed before the door opened, but he couldn't see who it was from his sprawled position. He decided to let whoever it was believe he was still unconscious and besides, his head hurt every time he moved. Whoever it was stood silently for a moment then stepped toward into his field of view.

He smiled at the sight of Naomi.

She held a tray with a pitcher, glass and other items. Sitting it on the dresser, she poured a glass of water. Turning toward him, her eyes caught his and she smiled. "How are you?"

"Head hurts."

She nodded. "It will pass." She handed him the glass of water and a tablet from the tray. "This will help." She waited while he swallowed, then said, "You are not a Nephilim."

"No. Just a man." Talking hurt his head. "How long have I been out?"

"Less than thirty minutes."

"Are we safe?"

She shook her head. "Not yet. The police and Ferren are in pursuit, but Mara is staying ahead of them."

*Started the day a prosperous business man and ended it a fugitive. Slowly he sat up. Definitely not my best day.* "Is Mara hooked to the ship's systems?"

"Ah, yes. I...I helped her connect." Her face flushed. "I didn't know she had an implant."

Justin nodded. "A present from our former owner." He reached out his arm. "Help me."

He put his arm around Naomi's shoulders and they walked out.

Naomi helped onto the ship's bridge. He'd been here several times while his crews worked on the yacht, but never while the ship was in flight. Even preoccupied with his pursuers and a throbbing head, the compartment was impressive. Shaped like an egg, the narrowest part of the room was toward the bow and opposite from where Justin stood at the entrance. Visual displays covered the bulkheads of the forward half. Just below these images were half-a-dozen workstations. At the center of the room was a captain's chair with a desk-like control panel arching in front of it.

Justin walked past the captain's chair to the forward end of the room. Mara lay in what appeared to be a pod-like reclining chair, arms beside her, eyes closed. Her general look gave the appearance of someone asleep, but Justin knew better. Optical fibers connected to the implant on the back of her skull linked her brain to the ship's helm, navigation and engineering systems.

"Mara," he called softly as his eyes darted about the room.

A holographic image formed on the right side of the captain's chair. "How are you doing brother?"

"I'm alive." He stepped in the direction of her image, but plopped into the captain's chair. "Where are we headed?"

"Just away at the moment." She pointed to a display showing aft sensors. "The nearest ship is a police cruiser the other is the Acheron."

*Ferren.* "Are they gaining on us?"

She nodded. "Got any ideas? They'll be in firing range in less than twelve minutes."

"Then we need a plan, a place to go, in less than eleven."

"Justin," Naomi said softly, "I know where we could go."

They both looked at her.

"I have not been…ah…." Naomi bit her lip. "I have not been entirely honest with you."

"Yeah, I know," he said without emotion.

Mara looked at Justin, her eyes wide. "You knew she was lying and…"

"Not right now, Mara. Go on Naomi."

"The man I was traveling with, Dr. Carl Saul…well, that was not his name and he was not my father—he was my creator."

## Chapter 8

"Creator?" Even though it was merely a holographic simulation, Mara's eyes seemed to fix like beacons on Naomi.

Justin's head sank into his hands. *I'll be glad when this day is over.* Gently he rubbed his temple. "What do you mean, Naomi?"

"Dr. Galen, that was his real name, was not taking me to Gatewai, he was taking me to a jump gate in the Spitzer system. I had never heard of the star before we left Earth."

Justin smiled knowingly. "Yesterday you said you were from Epsilon."

Her face flushed. "Dr. Galen was from Epsilon."

"Okay, but why were you traveling to Spitzer?"

"Galen said there were people on the other side of the jump that could hide me."

Mara's eyes flared. "Most of those gates haven't been used since the Titanomachy war—over four hundred years ago."

"Navsys on," Justin commanded. He turned to the console before him and mumbled, "Dr. Galen was taking you to Spitzer." Tapping his finger on the holographic map, he brought up the appropriate region of space. The display zoomed in and annotations appeared over several celestial bodies. "Spitzer is a white, dwarf star. The system has one gas giant and two rocky planetoids." He shook his head. "No habitable planets."

"Are you actually thinking about going there?" Mara raised her holographic eyebrow incredulously.

Justin again tapped his finger on the holographic map. "Do you have a better plan?"

"Well...." She turned to Naomi. "Did you say 'hide?' Why did you need to hide?"

The holographic image of a uniformed man appeared to the left of the captain's chair, opposite of Mara. He seemed to look Justin in the eye as he said, "Surfeit, decelerate and prepare to be boarded. Comply or we will open fire."

A flash of light swept the bridge and alarms sounded.

Justin's eyes locked on the fireball just ahead.

The words 'fugitive' and 'Titan' echoed in Justin's mind. He glanced at the display then silenced the alarms. "That was a shot across our bow. The next one will be into our engines."

Naomi's stared at the Navigation display. "What do we do?"

Justin felt his every muscle tense. Mara's eyes remained calm, but fixed on him. He could feel fear from both and see it on Naomi's face. Purposely he gave a casual shrug in answer to her question and took a slow deep breath and turned to Mara. "Do you have a better destination than Spitzer?"

Mara shook her head.

In the most confident voice he could muster he said, "Set course for Spitzer."

Mara nodded. Her image faded, blinked then snapped back to full intensity. "The course is set. I sure hope we find a working gate when we get there." She pointed to displays in front of Justin. "We won't have enough fuel to jump to another system after we arrive." A restraining harness slid across the real Mara as the holographic one said, "Strap in everyone. I'm going to need them off our tail." She gestured toward the pursuing ships.

Justin clicked his belt into place just as the thrusters roared, pushing him deep into the seat. The ship zigged one way as he zagged into the harness. Another wild turn and the police fell far behind, but Ferren's ship, the Acheron, continued to gain. Mara fired the retros, throwing Justin forward into the harness.

Their pursuer shot past.

Thrusters blazed as the Surfeit dashed off at a right angle from the Acheron.

"On your order Captain." Mara turned and waited for his command.

There was no hint of sarcasm at the word, "captain" and just for a moment, he marveled at how such an intelligent and talented woman had followed him all these years. "Jump."

The stars slid into one bright mass off the bow as Justin tried to gulp air, but he couldn't breathe. Abruptly he felt weightless and disoriented as the ship crossed the event horizon. The next instant he slammed hard into his harness and gasped.

"Jump complete." Mara smiled. "The vortex collapsed behind us before any ships could follow."

Justin took a deep draft of air and forced a smile. "How long till we arrive at Spitzer?"

"Just over Fifty-seven hours."

*When we get there all we need to do is find the gate and hope the ancient thing works.* Fatigue flowed over him. There were a thousand questions he needed answered, but, for now, there was only one thing he wanted to do. Looking at Mara he asked, "When will you need to eat and…ah go…"

"As soon as I do a ship wide systems check, I'll disconnect. Flying through subspace is easy."

He nodded. "I'll be in my room," he said walking from the bridge.

\* \* \*

The room was dark when he awoke. Justin felt his head and smiled. It didn't hurt. For a moment he struggled to remember the name of the ship he was on. "Surfeit lights, normal." The pitcher and glass that Naomi had brought him remained on the dresser. He stood, filled the cup and drank deeply. A glance in the mirror drew a moan as he rubbed the deep stubble of his beard and attempted to straighten his tousled hair. *Hopeless.* As he dressed he struggled to understand how the fall from respected businessman to fugitive had occurred so quickly. *I need answers.* With that resolve he marched from the compartment.

Someone had latched the door to the bridge open. The voices of the women greeted him as he approached the hatch. Stepping into the compartment he noticed a table had been setup at the rear with coffee and food. He grabbed some cheese as he passed.

"How do you feel?" Naomi asked.

"Much better." He looked about the bridge then back at Mara. Stepping forward he touched her on the arm.

Mara nodded. "Yes, this is the real me."

"What's our status?" he asked, then consumed the cheese.

Mara shrugged. "We're on auto-pilot still traversing the wormhole. When we get to Spitzer we'll be low on fuel."

Justin nodded. Those problems were still some hours in the future. He turned to Naomi. "Yesterday you said that Dr. Galen was not your father, that he was your creator. What did you mean? Are you a clone?"

Mara frowned. "I've already asked. She won't answer."

"It is complicated." She looked at both of them, "If I had to tell, I wanted to do so only once."

Justin stared at her. "Okay, let's get started."

Naomi sighed deeply. "I told you his name was Dr. Carl Saul, but that was just part of the cover story. Like I said his real name was Dr. Luke Galen." Tears welled in her eyes. "He was a good man."

Touched by her emotion, Justin sat beside her and took her hand.

"I do not know where to start."

He squeezed her hand gently. "We have time. Start at the beginning."

She nodded and wiped her eyes. "Okay," she sighed. "Twenty years ago an imperial warship detected a cloaked vessel running at high speed in the restricted zone between the CFS and the empire. Thinking it was a CFS spy ship they attacked and disabled it."

Mara held up a hand. "Do we need the history lesson? Just start with why you call this Galen guy your creator."

"This is where my story begins."

Mara looked confused.

"Go on," Justin said.

"When imperial marines boarded the ship the crew destroyed most of the onboard systems and vented the atmosphere."

Mara's eyes widened. "They committed suicide?"

Naomi nodded.

"But I still don't get it. What does all this have to do with you?"

"Unfortunately everything." Taking in a deep breath she continued. "Imperial Intelligence determined that the crew were Titans."

Justin's breath caught in his throat and he felt Mara's surprise wash over him. *I could use a drink. A good strong one.* He examined Naomi's face, trying to grasp the fullness of what she had implied. "Are you saying that you're a Titan?"

"In a sense."

"No," Mara said flatly. "That's something you either are or you aren't." Her eyes locked on Naomi as she slowly stood. "What are you?"

"Calm down, Sis. If she were some genetically-enhanced murderer, we'd be dead already."

"They were cunning."

"Remember," he said gesturing toward his chest, "I might be a Titan."

She shook her head and moved to the side and slightly behind Naomi, "Whatever you are, you're not a genocidal, killing machine."

"Let's hear her out."

Mara's hand slid into a pocket. "Okay." Slowly she moved back toward the bulkhead.

Naomi continued. "Remember that the Titans were created as soldiers and support laborers to protect Earth from the Grays. After their surrender, EarthGov ordered the Titans to return to base for resettlement."

"They refused," Justin nodded recalling the history, "and sent the ten plagues against the people of Earth."

"That was the start of the Titanomachy War." Mara said flatly.

"Any Titans they captured were burned at the stake," Justin shuddered as he imagined flames inching closer to his body.

"Before the war was over, billons had died." Mara sighed. "EarthGov and the Confederation collapsed and the Nephilim were victorious."

Naomi nodded. "The Nephilim defeated the Titans at the Battle of Earth and eventually were able to restore order but everyone remembered the horror of the war, the famine and unrest, and sought to guard against it. They ordered the scientists of the empire to create a Titan-like army for them, but Earth scientists have not been able to isolate the DNA sequences that give the Titan their powers. "Many scientists have paid for that failure with their life."

"Okay, I see." Justin said. "The scientists failed until twenty years ago."

Naomi nodded.

Mara shook her head. "I still don't understand. What has all that got to do with you?"

"One of the bodies from the cloaked ship provided viable DNA. The Nephilim were able to advance their plans."

"So you are..."

"I am a clone and the prototype for the new army of the Nephilim."

## Chapter 9

Mara stared at Naomi for several moments then, in a flat, emotionless voice said, "I've got to admit, you don't look like a genetically-enhanced monster."

Naomi eyed her carefully. "I do not think of myself as a monster, but I am strong, fast, and," her voice lowered to a growl, "trained to kill."

"Stop it, ladies." A wry smile crossed Justin's face. "And I thought I was going crazy. You're telepathic too."

"Yes and telekinetic."

"So," he gestured toward his head, "was it just you communicating with me in the passageway or…"

"No. To communicate like that we both must be telepathic. And you are strongly telekinetic. When you threw me up against the wall with your mind I could not break free."

"What?" Mara asked. "When did that happen?"

Justin ignored his sister. "I'm not in control of these powers. How did you learn to use your psychic abilities?"

"Dr. Galen taught me from texts recovered from the Titans. Anu and Enlil and other Nephilim would often watch these sessions."

Mara's eyes fixed on Naomi, "You've actually seen Nephilim?"

"Many times during my psychic training and occasionally during my physical training."

"I always believed…we were taught that they were myths." Mara's mouth hung open, but for a moment, no words came forth. "It was just a story created by those in power to keep power."

"They are real."

Justin shook his head. "Apparently not everything taught in the CFS is true."

Mara's eyes widened with fear. "They are so going to hunt us down and kill us both."

Naomi nodded. "I think that is so and since I have fled they will kill me also."

Justin rubbed his face. *First they'll take DNA samples—then they'll kill us.* "We need to find that jump gate." And I hope it works and whoever is on the other side doesn't want us dead. "How long until we arrive at Spitzer?"

"About forty-six hours," Mara said without looking at the console.

Rubbing his chin Justin said, "I always thought of myself as a Norm." He glanced at Naomi. "Neither of us asked for this, but we are what we are—Titans."

"I do not consider myself a Titan."

He tilted his head back. "What would you call yourself then?"

Naomi shrugged. "Your friend."

Justin smiled, "Good enough for now." He had more questions, but for now that was enough to mull over. "I'll take the next watch. You two get some rest."

The women stared at each other. Apparently neither wanted to be the first to leave. After several seconds Naomi shrugged and departed.

"Call me if you need anything," Mara said.

He nodded and she walked away.

Justin moved about the bridge, reading the displays and becoming familiar with the location of the various controls. Normally the FTL drive would power all ship systems, but Mara had it balanced to use the absolute minimum anti-matter fuel to maintain a stable wormhole around them. It was only then that he noticed the controls for the small fission reactor. Usually it served only as a backup power supply but, she had it running at maximum. It would not extend their range significantly, but it would help. *Good job Mara.*

After several minutes he sat in the captain's chair. Leaning forward, he rested his chin on his hand. The Navsys showed their progress as they raced toward the Spitzer system, but even with Mara's good piloting they would arrive low on fuel. *We'll need to find the jump gate quickly. Jump gate? I don't even know for sure there is a jump gate in the system.* He shook his head. *Even if there is, it's hundreds of years old. It probably won't work. And Spitzer is a white dwarf, there aren't any habitable planets.* Leaning back in the chair, he rubbed his face with both hands.

Naomi words flashed through his mind, "And you are strongly telekinetic." He recalled how he held Naomi against the wall with the crumbled gun at her feet. He remembered Ferren hanging in the air.

Memories of Garrett, the man who had bought him and Mara, the man who had treated him like a son and taught him the salvage business, rolled through Justin's mind. On that last, terrible, day they had walked down the passageway to the cargo bays.

"I've got to cut costs," Garrett had said.

Justin knew that work had been slow and nodded.

"I'm going to sell several workers, including Mara."

"No." Justin shouted.

"Remember your place," Garrett said sharply and picked up his pace down the passageway.

Justin followed, pleaded and then begged.

"With that implant I had put in her skull she is worth more than all the other slaves I'm selling," He stopped and lowered his voice. "Look when things pick up I'll get you someone, but for now that's my decision." Garrett turned and walked into an empty cargo bay.

Justin waited at a portal as rage boiled within him. *I wish you were dead.* With eyes fixed on the large bay doors, he imagined opening them. *Breathe vacuum.* He spit the words out as a curse. Metal creaked and popped. The door blew away. With a whoosh, Garrett shot into the void of space.

Though he had no idea how he was to blame, Justin announced his guilt to the authorities. They assured him he was not responsible. The bay door was old. The metal was weak. It was all just a terrible accident; he had not murdered the man who, in his will, had freed him and given him the salvage business. In the years that followed, Justin almost convinced himself of his innocence, but now he knew he had killed Garrett with a thought.

Images of Mara in the escape pod with him years before flashed into his mind. When the alarms sounded he screamed and cried for his mother, but she did not come. When his ears began popping, he knew what he must do. Putting his shoulder to the pod door, he shut it. Moments later, his mother banged at the portal. With Mara, he struggled to open the door. He failed and because of his failure his mother died. He had killed her—not with his mind, but with a bad decision. *My decisions are going to cause the death of Mara and Naomi in mere hours. My mother...Garrett...Mara...Naomi. I kill the people I care for most.*

Consumed by his thoughts Justin didn't notice Mara walk in until she stood before him.

"What are you doing here? Get some sleep."

She shook her head. "I can't. I've got too much on my mind. She sat. "I thought you might want company."

Justin could see and feel that she was tense. "Sure. Keep me company."

For several moments she stared at the displays. "Will we find the jump gate and get somewhere safe?"

"Yeah. Sure," he said with a nod. *No. You've probably followed me to your death.*

Mara looked at him hopefully, but fear lingered in her eyes.

"I'm working on some plans and ideas for when we arrive at Spitzer." It was all a lie, but he had always felt the need to keep his inner doubts to himself.

She smiled and he felt her fear abate. "I'll take the watch if you want some food."

"Food?" He looked at the table at the back of the bridge. The coffee pot was empty and the counter was bare. "I *am* hungry. I think the last real meal I ate was the dinner with you and Naomi."

"I put our stuff in the private galley." As he stood, she gestured toward the displays. "You didn't change any settings while I was gone did you?"

Forcing a frown he said, "Are you afraid I might have messed up something?"

"No," she said unconvincingly, "but I am the better pilot."

"That you are," he said with a smile. "I didn't touch a thing."

Justin first peeked into the utilitarian crew galley, a small gray room with a single, long, table running down the middle, then headed up one deck to the larger and more comfortable private dining room. Walking into the kitchen his stomach growled in anticipation. He sighed at what he found. Ration boxes and crackers filled the pantry. *Let's see.* A frown spread across his face. *I'll have artificially flavored soy protein meat substitute.* He opened the package and removed a square block that somewhat resembled beef. *And radiated vegetables and juice and a ration of potato flakes.*

\*　　　\*　　　\*

Filling, but tasteless. He patted his full stomach as he headed back toward the bridge. *I ate rations for years and lived, I guess I can do it again.*

Passing the crew galley he smelled food cooking and poked his head in. Naomi, with her hair pulled back tight, was stirring a pot while keeping an eye on something in the processor.

He stepped in. "There's a nicer galley one deck up."

"Oh" she said with a start. "Yes, I know." She looked around. "I felt more comfortable in this one." Then she quickly turned back to the food.

Breathing deeply he took in the aroma that filled the small room. "Is that soup? It smells good."

Talking over her shoulder she said, "The crew stocked their pantry with some fresh food."

*Of course,* he grinned, *the crew would stock their galley first.*

"I'm cooking enough for both of us. I figured you would be hungry."

He smiled. *Stuffed.* "Famished."

"Good." Her face seemed to glow. "Sit down. It will be done in a moment."

Naomi laid before him a tray with bowls of fresh salad, soup and mixed vegetables. Beside it, she set a dish of identical square blobs of mystery meat.

"It looks very nice." *I just wish I wasn't full.*

"The meat is the cheap package stuff, but I made the soup from fresh carrots, celery, beans—anything I could find really."

Justin let his eyes linger on her face. "Great."

For several minutes Naomi dug into her food while Justin nibbled, smiled, and lavished compliments.

"What did Dr. Galen tell you about the Spitzer jump gate?"

"Nothing, really."

"Where it is in the solar system?"

Mouth full, she shrugged and shook her head.

Justin slowly let his breath out. "I was afraid you would say that. *Our lives depend on finding an old jump gate that somehow is still working.* "I'll need to get Mara to plot a search pattern."

She swallowed then said, "I think Mara is afraid of me."

He agreed.

"I am glad that I do not frighten you."

Poking at the lettuce, he said, "I know you're not going to hurt me." *That came out wrong.* "And besides, I can take care of myself." *That didn't sound right either.*

She shrugged. "Does Mara believe I will hurt her?"

He tapped his hand on the table several times. "She accepts that you were made from Titan DNA." He paused. "Everything we know says they were an idea that went badly wrong. Hundreds of millions died as the war went on."

"But she is not afraid of you."

He sighed. "I'm not sure that she believes I'm a Titan." *I'm not entirely sure that I do.* "But she knows me like, well, a sister—even though we're not."

She nodded.

"You don't seem surprised."

"That she is not your sister?"

He nodded. "We've never told anyone the truth."

"You showed me the truth in the passageway. Remember, just before you threw me up against the wall…"

She had stared at him and suddenly memories flashed through his mind. "That was you?" He wiggled his fingers over his head. "What? You probed my mind?"

"I had to know the truth."

"How much did you learn about me?"

She smiled coyly.

His face flushed.

"I had to know for sure that you were not a Nephilim or...." She let her sentence die.

*Oh, this is so unfair.* Desperately he recalled what had passed through his mind. He remembered imagining Naomi in the dress that Mara wore to dinner and staring at her when she was first brought in, unconscious. He cringed. "Do you remember everything?"

She giggled. "My recall of your memories will fade over the next few days, well, most of them will."

His face was still hot as he remembered what had flashed through his mind. *Yeah, I can imagine which ones won't be fading.* His heart pounded in his ears as he sat in silence. Desperately he wanted to change the subject. "So, other than embarrassing me, what did the Nephilim plan for you?"

Her eyes drifted to the table. Her demeanor sobered. "Over the years they told me of several missions they wanted accomplished."

"Such as...."

Without emotion in either face or voice she said, "My first standing order was to kill any Titans I encountered."

## Chapter 10

Justin's muscles tensed. "Uh...you can understand how that statement might make me a bit nervous, can't you?"

Naomi nibbled at her food. "Because you believe you are a Titan?"

Sensing no malice from her, he nodded. "My abilities pretty well establish my ancestry."

"You're not like any Titan I've ever read about."

He tried to smile. *Neither are you.*

"That day you nearly killed Ferren, I thought...." She smiled and shook her head. "It was silly but, I thought you were a Nephilim."

Justin managed to grin. "You only had two choices, Nephilim or Titan, why is one choice sillier than the other?"

"The Nephilim seemed to avoid me. Usually they were so far away I could barely sense their presence. On those rare occasions when they came a little closer, all I could sense was cold darkness."

Justin pushed the now empty plate aside. "What do you mean?"

"Unfeeling maliciousness and their minds seemed old. Older than anyone I've ever met."

"How old?"

"I don't know. You did not ask them questions—you obeyed. The Nephilim are supposed to be the saviors of humankind, but all I ever sensed was coldness and once…"

"What?"

"Only once did one ever get close enough for me to see into their mind. It radiated evil like a fire." She reached out, took his plate, and set it on her now empty one. "I have never sensed evil from you. It was silly of me to think you were Nephilim."

"Well then I guess I'd rather be a young, good Titan." He Stared into her eyes and was glad she was there. "So, when you fled from the Nephilim, it was because you didn't want to kill Titans?" *I hope, I really hope.*

"No." She took in a deep breath. "The idea that I am made from Titan DNA is disgusting to me and I could have, would have, completed my mission to destroy them."

Deliberately repeating himself he said, "You can understand how that might make me a bit nervous, can't you?"

She looked confused

"So, would you kill me? Apparently, I'm a Titan."

Frustration covered her face, but sadness filled her voice. "Our common DNA gives us abilities, but it is not what makes us Titans. They were a badly carried out plan, a hateful and cruel creation that attempted to enslave the human race." Staring at the bulkhead, Naomi paused. "There is no hate in you, no cruelty. You've protected Mara. That is why I asked to come with you. I knew you would help me." She took a deep breath. When she continued, anger tinged her voice. "I fled from the Nephilims for many reasons, but when I did, I stopped obeying their orders."

Dinner was finished in silence.

\*     \*     \*

Suffocation. Just before they crossed the event horizon Justin gulped air, but it didn't help, it still felt like drowning. Disorientation and weightlessness immediately followed.

Suddenly slammed into the harness he gasped for air. *I hate FTL travel.*

The image of Mara seemed to exhale and then smile. "We're back in standard space. All systems normal."

Justin hoped that the contents of his stomach would remain where they belonged. He breathed deeply. "Let's find that jump gate."

Naomi looked down at a panel. "Starting sensor sweeps."

"Which of those search patterns you told me about will work best?"

Mara spoke up, "I can put us in an elliptical orbit that will allow us to search the system using no fuel."

"How long would it take to complete the search?"

"Just over thirty-two years."

He grinned "I'd like to find it sooner than that. We'll need to use the little fuel we have left."

Mara shook her head. "The two planetoids are on opposite sides of the system. We don't have enough fuel to reach all the planets."

"Then we need another plan. NavSys on." Justin watched intently as the various planets, asteroids and comets appeared before him. Slowly he moved around the display occasionally pausing to stare at some point in space. With the image of the gas giant before him he stopped. After several moments he gave a nod. "If I were going to hide a jump gate this is where I would do it."

Mara stepped beside him. "A ringed gas giant, a dozen moons…"

"An abundance of sensor targets," Naomi added.

He folded his arms across his chest. "And plenty of Lagrange points."

"Lagrange points?" Naomi asked.

"Places where the gravitational pull of the star, planet and a moon balance out." He grinned. "The jump gate would stay in a fixed position."

"Oh. In the empire they are called libration points."

"Whatever you call them," his eyes darted between the women, "we need to find and scan those spots."

\*     \*     \*

Justin tapped the display. *Location 39 negative*. He rubbed his tired eyes. *Twelve more to check*. With the many large moons around the gas giant it had taken hours just to plot the locations and it was taking much longer to scan them all.

Naomi snored softly in the corner.

*Maybe there is no gate*. He walked to the food table and selected what, hours ago, had been a muffin, but now was as dry as a cracker. He washed it down with lukewarm coffee.

Naomi snored loudly and turned on her side.

Mara appeared in the center of the bridge. "Mmmh." She stared intently as her head slid closer to the sensor console.

"Did you find something?"

She stared at the panel for a moment then hesitantly said, "Yes."

Justin walked casually toward her. *Why does the hologram of Mara stare at the console?*

She shouted, "Yes!"

"Huh?" Naomi sat up.

Justin ran to Mara's side and peered at the readings. There was something out there. Quickly he directed the sensor data to the holographic display and watched. "Two? There's two objects."

Mara, smiled. "I'll have a course plotted in moments. Slowing to 35,000 KPH."

As they approached, it became clear that both a derelict ship and a jump gate slowly orbited the Lagrange point. The steel ring, just visible at that distance, but big enough for a warship to pass through, formed the gate. The power source, a fusion reactor, glowed at the end of a long shaft extending from the circle.

"The gate has power, but I don't detect any power sources on the ship. Why do you think it was left here?" Naomi asked.

He shrugged. *Maybe the crew died there when the gate didn't work—just like we might.* Images of some future explorer finding the jump gate with two ships nearby, blazed through his mind.

"We're on approach. ETA, 20 minutes."

As they drew closer Naomi's gaze fixed on the sensor readouts. "The ship is a frigate. Very old design." She paused, looked up at Justin, and continued. "Probably from the Titanomachy War. The FTL engines are gone, but I can still see missile launchers and particle weapons."

Justin watched the image as it grew slowly larger. "We should see if the gate responds. Send the activation sequence."

Mara nodded.

"When you're ready go ahead and send it."

She turned. Worry etched her face. "I already did."

Everyone watched the main screen while nothing happened.

That confirms it. The gate doesn't work. He sighed.

"What are we going to do?" Naomi asked.

Justin waved his hand for her to stop. "I'm thinking." *Antimatter fuel is all but exhausted so we can't jump to another system. We can try to fix the gate. Surfeit has a skiff.* He shook his head. *No spacesuits—we can't fix it.*

The objects ahead now filled the main screen. "Mara, reduce the display magnification."

"Display magnification set to normal and reducing approach velocity to 10,000 KPH."

As Mara continued to slow their approach, Justin attempted to come up with a workable plan and failed. He glanced at both of them, but not wanting them to see the worry that he felt, avoided eye contact. He walked to the food table and, while nibbling on anything that presented itself, he continued to formulate plans in vain.

"Why is it warm?" Naomi asked.

Confused, Justin turned and saw Naomi holding her pendant in her hands.

"Because it's been against your skin," Mara sneered.

Naomi rolled her eyes. "No. It is warmer than that." She cupped it in her hands and stared down at it. Her head popped up. "Surfeit lights, off." Again she looked down into her cupped hands and, for a moment, her face was illuminated by a golden glow. Slowly she pulled her fingers away revealing the pulsating pendant.

Justin watched. Not only was it pulsating, it grew brighter with each pulse. He returned the lights to normal.

Mara's eyes went from Justin to Naomi, "What is that thing?"

"I don't know. Dr. Galen gave it to me and empathically told me to keep it." Naomi took it from her neck and laid it on her lap.

Justin stared at the glowing orb. "We can be sure of two things: Dr. Galen gave it to you for a reason, and somehow it's connected with this gate." He walked about the bridge, deep in thought, then stopped and watched the pendant for several moments. "It pulsates every two seconds."

Mara gave him a perplexed look. "So?"

With a shrug he continued his walk about the bridge. Why would it start warming and pulsating only when we got here?

Mara turned to Justin, "We're about as close to the gate as I want to get."

Without pausing his slow walk about the bridge he mumbled, "Put us in orbit around the point."

Seconds later Mara announced, "Forward momentum zero. Thrusters at station-keeping."

He finished another unhurried lap around the bridge as a smile spread slowly. "How many ways can you send energy from one place to another?"

Both women shrugged.

He waved his hand toward the pendant. "Less than an hour ago we thought it was just jewelry, but it's not. Energy, in some form, has activated it."

Mara leaned back in her chair. "You're thinking either the gate or ship is sending it power?"

"Yes. I'm sure Dr. Galen knew the pendant would activate when they approached…."

"Look!" Naomi pointed to the screen, her eyes wide. Lights flashed on the derelict.

"Sensors indicate environmental systems are turning on," Mara declared. "I'm detecting infrared radiation."

As the derelict's docking bay opened. The lights of the ship and the pendant now pulsated in unison. "Apparently someone wants us to pay them a visit."

## Chapter 11

Mara pulled Justin aside before he entered the skiff's airlock. "I'm not sure this is a good idea."

He sighed and stepped inside the hatch. "We already talked about it. I thought we should take the pendant to the ship and Naomi insisted she go with it."

"No, not that...well really more than that." She paused. "Is going over there a good idea?"

He smiled weakly. "It's a lot better than sitting here until our food and fuel runs out." *But I wish I had a weapon for this trip.* He squeezed her hand. "We'll be back in minutes."

Mara handed him a commlink. "I'm going to reconnect to the ship—just in case we need to move fast."

He nodded. *But, where can we go?*

She smiled weakly and shut the airlock hatch.

From the pilot seat, Naomi looked over her shoulder as he entered the rear of the skiff. The low light of the control panel and the glow from the pendant dangling outside her blouse, softly illuminated her face. For a moment Justin drank the pleasing picture.

She smiled. "You need to seal the hatch."

"Oh, yes." He turned and did so. "Can you fly this thing?"

"Yes. I am a good pilot."

He looked at the six, empty, passenger seats in the cramped compartment and smiled, "Should I sit back here?"

She gestured toward the co-pilot seat, "We should get started."

As the skiff glided toward the frigate, Justin was glad he sat up front. The cockpit window provided a panoramic view. Instantly he observed a counter clockwise swirl on the planet before him. It was a storm disrupting the crimson, orange, brown and white bands that otherwise encircled the giant world. Off the starboard bow, two icy silver moons slid by in the endless sashay of the solar system, while off the port side the arc of the encircling rings dipped below his view. A host of stars served as the backdrop for the grand vista.

"Usually we see this as a hologram or an image on a screen," he said, still focused on the spectacle. "I've never seen anything like this before in real life."

Naomi glanced at him and smiled, "In the Earth system there is a planet called Saturn that is very similar." She returned to the ship controls. "ETA at the derelict two minutes."

Slowly he scanned the view. "I want to remember this and paint it someday."

The skiff touched down in the bay and air filled the compartment. As she exited the craft Naomi crossed her arms. "This ship is cold."

His smiled at her frosty breath and nodded.

"Which way should we go?"

The etching wobbled back and forth. "Look at your pendant."

She took the chain from her neck and held it in her hand like a compass. After a moment, she pointed to the other side of the skiff toward the bow of the ship.

Walking briskly in the cold they came to the far side of the craft. Painted high on the bulkhead before them was a double helix shield with crossed swords.

Justin stared at the emblem, but raised the commlink to his lips. "Mara, we're onboard. It's a Titan ship."

"Get out, now! We'll come up with some other plan."

Fear tempted him.

Naomi shook her head. "Whoever created this pendant and left the ship here wanted people to find this place and there could be food and fuel onboard."

He agreed. "Let's be quick."

Several minutes later, as they trotted down a passageway, Naomi peered down at the orb and pointed ahead.

Justin glanced at the pendant. The golden glow was now constant. The etching stood out in sharp contrast. "I think we're close."

Breathing heavily, they approached an entryway with two sliding doors. The same two intersecting arcs that created the simple outline of a fish on Naomi's pendant were etched on one side while on the other was the double helix coat of arms.

Justin continued toward the doors.

Naomi stopped five meters from them.

They did not open.

Glancing down at the glowing orb she said, "Our path is through that door."

The commlink crackled. "Justin, come in." Tension sprang from Mara's voice.

"What's the problem?" He continued to look for a way to open the hatch.

"Two ships just entered normal space at the edge of the system."

"Can you identify?"

"Not at this distance."

"Well don't worry. They could be anybody, miners, explorers, researchers. They could be lost. Who knows why they're here." He didn't believe that, but it almost sounded plausible. "Have they seen us?"

"I don't think so. We're using minimal power so we're not much of a sensor target."

"Okay. Let me know when you have more information."

Justin continued to look for a switch, knob, or lever, that would allow them to pass. After several moments he glanced back at Naomi still standing several meters behind. "Is something wrong?"

Naomi didn't move. "The ships…. It is probably Ferren, and others, looking for us."

Continuing to search along the wall he nodded in agreement.

"The gate may not work…"

He gestured toward the door. "It might if we get inside."

"I need to say something—just in case."

Frustrated, he slowly turned and without emotion asked, "What?"

The radio crackled again. "Justin, come in."

"What?" He didn't attempt to hide his annoyance.

"They're broadcasting an order for us to surrender. It's Ferren's ship, the Acheron, and a police cruiser."

"How much fuel do we have?"

"Not enough to get away. What do we do?"

Justin leaned against the bulkhead. "Are they on an approach vector?"

"No, they're in a search pattern."

He shook his head. "They haven't found us." *Yet.* "But if we activate the gate you can bet they'll jump right on top of us."

Looking at Naomi, he asked, "What were you saying?"

"Never mind," She said coolly. "Let's figure out how to open that door." For the first time she moved right in front. It slid open.

Justin swept the small room with his eyes. Consoles and displays lined the bulkheads. A terminal stood in the middle.

Naomi stepped into the compartment.

Immediately the doors moved to close. Justin leapt through as they did, landing with a thud on the deck. He picked himself up as the holographic image of a man in uniform appeared.

"Greetings. I am the sentinel for this gate. If you wish to pass through come forward and be identified." The man gestured toward the panel in front of him.

Justin followed his motion. Located at the center of the controls was the contoured depression in the shape of a left hand. Before he could say anything, Naomi placed her hand in it.

"Ouch! It pricked my finger," she said rubbing it.

The sentinel's eyes fixed on Naomi standing at the console. He seemed to ponder something about her. Then text streamed down the screen beside him.

Justin stepped closer attempting to read it, but it wasn't words, merely long strings of letters that rapidly scrolled down.

"My DNA?" Naomi said, staring at the screen.

When the cascade of letters stopped the display ended with two lines of text.

**Subject: Female.**

*I noticed.*

**DNA sequence: 84-11. Specialty: Mobile Infantry Pilot.**

A slight smile spread across the face of the hologram. "Welcome, sister Titan. What is your rank?"

"Sister?" She looked at Justin. "Rank?"

He shrugged.

"Lieutenant?"

He nodded. "There is another person on the bridge. Come forward and be identified."

Justin placed his hand in the outline and felt the sting at the end of his index finger.

Again the letters flowed in rapid succession.

**Subject: Male**

**DNA sequence: 133-37.  Specialty: Naval Line Officer.**

"Welcome, brother Titan. What is your rank?"

In some corner of his mind, he had held out hope that it was all some misunderstanding, that he was not a Titan, and could explain what had happened to Ferren and resume his ordinary norm life. But that last thread of hope had been consumed by the words "Welcome, brother Titan."

He glanced at Naomi and was thankful that if he must travel down this frightful road he had her and Mara's companionship.

"What is your rank, brother Titan?"

*Brother Titan?* His eyes darted from the sentinel to Naomi. He had no desire to be outranked by her so, with a wry smile in her direction, said, "Admiral."

The sentinel saluted. A holographic display of the system appeared. Turning toward it he pointed, "There are three ships in the solar system, please identify friend and foe."

Justin quickly did so.

"Do you wish me to engage the enemy?"

"We need to return to our ship and jump. Provide covering fire as we do."

"Yes, Admiral." Again the sentinel gestured to a console. "Please insert the key."

"Key?" Naomi asked.

Justin pointed to the chain in her hand. "Your pendant."

She placed the golden orb in a slot on the terminal.

"Coordinates entered...Destination locked...Activating gate...You may remove the key."

Naomi retrieved her pendant, but her eyes remained fixed on the sentinel.

"Justin," Mara shouted over the commlink, "The gate! A wormhole is forming!"

"We're coming," Justin shouted into the commlink. "Be ready to jump." He ran toward the door, but stopped short when it did not open. He looked back at Naomi.

She had not moved.

"We've got to go."

"Of course." Her gaze slid from the silent sentinel to Justin. "It all makes sense now. "Dr. Galen knew I was made from Titan DNA and figured they would hide me." Her mouth hung agape. "The Titans must be on the other side of the gate."

"Ferren and the police are on this side."

She remained fixed like a statue.

He breathed deeply. "What chance do we have here?" He walked up to her and gently took her hand. "Ferren and the police will kill us."

Tears welled in her eyes. "The Titans..."

"Didn't kill other Titans." He moved quickly to her and pulled her close. "Please, come with me. Whatever is on the other side we'll face it together." The door opened as they stepped forward. He urged her on as raced down the passageway, through the ship, and across the docking bay. The whoosh of missile launches and the crackle of particle beams greeted them as they ran up the ramp and into the skiff.

## Chapter 12

Explosive flashes and searing beams of light illuminated what, minutes ago, had been a tranquil scene.

Naomi eased the skiff out of the bay. Her eyes darted from the sensor console to the cockpit window. "Where is Surfeit?"

Quickly Justin scanned from port to starboard. He cursed and grabbed the commlink.

*Hiding.*

With Mara's single word echoing somehow in his head he knew the location of Surfeit as if he had moved the skiff. He turned to Naomi.

She nodded. "I heard her," and threw the craft into a high-speed 90-degree turn over the central portion of the frigate.

Justin struggled to clip his belt as Naomi, hugging the Titan ship, passed through a dip in the superstructure to the port side. Surfeit, illuminated by the reflected light of the planet, hovered close alongside.

As they approached, Surfeit rolled over, revealing the open docking bay.

Deftly, Naomi aligned the skiff with the mother ship.

A loud clank told Justin the docking clamps had locked in place. *Go! Through the gate—now.*

Thrusters roared.

Inertia flung Justin hard against the seat. Within moments came the flash and familiar sickness that signaled the event horizon.

Without a word, Naomi stood and hurried out.

He guessed why she rushed out and followed, hoping the queasiness in his stomach would soon pass.

Stepping onto the bridge Naomi shouted, "You communicated with us. *You* are telepathic." She stepped closer. "*You are one of them—a Titan.*"

Mara pulled a knife and pointed it at her. "So are you," she sneered.

"What are you doing, Mara! Put that away."

She lowered the knife, but kept it out.

Justin stepped between them and lifted his arms to fend them off. "Apparently we have a Titan family reunion on this ship."

"It makes sense now." Naomi smirked. "You were both on that ship as children. It must have been a Titan ship."

"You told her about that?"

"Sort of." Quickly he mulled Naomi's assertion. It seemed logical. If he were a Titan, Mara would probably be also. What use would the Titans have for norms? Facing her he asked, "How long have you known?"

She blinked and wiped her eyes, but the knife remained pointed in their direction. "I didn't know—for sure. Occasionally something strange would happen. I'd hear someone's thought...feel what they felt. But I dismissed it—until that night."

"What night?"

"When Ferren tried to take us. I called to you."

He remembered waking up with her voice shouting in his head. "Why didn't you tell me?"

A single tear rolled down her cheek. "Tell you I've become a freak and a murderer?"

Naomi shook her head. "You are not changing. You are what you have always been."

"The night I called you, the night I knew for sure that I was a Titan," she took a ragged breath, "only seconds later I murdered someone and then another and another." Tears welled in her eyes.

"You defended yourself. We all did what we had to do," Justin stepped toward her. "I tried to kill Ferren. I shot…."

"You didn't kill anyone," she flashed the knife at him.

"Sis, what are you doing? Drop the knife."

Haltingly, between gasping breaths and tearful sobs, her words came. "Titans are.. savages…test tube creations…heartless monsters…they killed millions."

Naomi shook her head. "That is what they were, but it is not what we are."

Justin nodded in agreement.

She took a deep breath and a calmness came to her face. "I'll never be a Titan." She placed the knifepoint against her chest and thrust.

\* \* \*

"How is she?" he asked.

"The external bleeding has stopped, but she punctured a lung and I am sure there is internal bleeding." Naomi shook her head. "I feel helpless. Any clinic could treat her wound." She sank into a chair. "It may be fatal."

He sighed deeply and wiped his eyes. *Hang on Sis.* "I'm hoping the Titans will help one of their own."

She frowned. "We are seeking safety and medical care amongst the worst mass murders in human history." She paused. Her eyes drifted down. "I can guess how Mara must have felt."

"And we have another problem. Surfeit, main screen on. Aft view."

Naomi approached and scrutinized the display. "A ship? There is another vessel in the wormhole?"

"The Acheron," he said with a nod. "They must have followed us in."

"Look here." She pointed to the pirate vessel's bow. "He was hit, but not bad enough to stop him. What do you think Ferren will do?"

"I don't believe he'll fire on us now, too risky. He could destabilize the wormhole and kill himself. He's greedy. If he captures us alive we'd probably fetch a much better price. He'll get as close as possible so when we return to normal space, he'll fire on our engines and thrusters."

"What is your plan?"

"When we exit the wormhole, we'll zigzag like crazy and hope the Titans don't like pirates."

With a frown, Naomi moved to the helm. "He is less than three kilometers behind us." She turned to face Justin. "It will be nearly impossible to evade his weapons."

*Yeah, I know, it isn't much of a plan.* "When the time comes, do your best." He stared at Ferren's ship. "Speaking of time, when will we return to normal space?"

She looked at the navigation and FTL controls. "Without knowing our destination, I can only estimate, but it won't be long—six hours maybe. You should get some sleep."

He nodded. "I'll check on Mara."

Justin awoke seated at the end of Mara's bed with his head resting against her foot. Slowly he stood rubbing his sore back and neck. Mara looked ghostly, but her quiet breathing assured him that she slept. *Stay with us, Sis. I'll get you help and find us a safe place.* With the promise firm in mind, he marched to the bridge.

As he stepped into the compartment, Ferren pointed his finger, "It's foolhardy to leave your bridge unattended."

Justin gasped.

"If you want to kill yourself, I can help, but I prefer to take you alive." He laughed uproariously.

Suddenly Justin noticed Naomi, eyes closed and motionless, standing out of the view of the communications camera. *How did you get on my ship?* He stepped slowly forward and then noticed a slight distortion of the pirates face. He sighed. *You're a hologram.*

Ferren seemed to read his mind and laughed again. With a sweep of his arm he said, "Sit down. We should talk."

"What about?" Justin directed his thoughts to Naomi. *What's going on?* But, there was no reply. He moved to the captain's chair and sat.

"I want you to surrender, of course."

"Why should I?"

"You're a Titan, we need to kill you."

Justin glanced at his shipmate, pressed mute on the console, and asked, "Naomi, what are you doing?"

Keeping her eyes closed, she shook her head.

Pressing mute once more, he caught the pirate in mid sentence.

"…talk about it. Oh, and I must withdraw my offer of marriage to your sister. You do understand."

Justin shook his head in disbelief. *You married to her? Never going to happen. She'd cut off body parts you haven't seen in years thanks to that fat belly.* "I've been thinking about that a lot lately." His voice dripped sarcasm. "I understand your situation, really I do. Why marry someone you're going to burn at the stake in a few days."

The pirate smiled. "Exactly. Now about your surrender," A pained expression crossed his face and he rubbed his bulbous chest. "I would prefer you make this easy."

"So, that's your terms? I surrender so you can kill me—and my sister?"

Ferren frowned and rubbed his left arm. "That slave you're so fond of might live. So, yes those are…"

"No." Justin ended the transmission. His face felt warm. *Does everyone know how I feel about Naomi?* Turning to her, he asked, "Is everything okay?"

For a moment, she stood like a statue, then with a sigh her shoulders slumped. "I was out of view when he called." She smiled mischievously. "I tried to give his overworked heart a good hard squeeze."

"Give him a heart attack?"

She grinned.

"You can do that?"

The grin slid away. "Apparently not at this distance."

Recalling Ferren rubbing his chest and arm he smiled. "I think he's lucky you stopped trying." He glanced at the controls. "How soon will we return to normal space?"

"Anytime now."

Minutes later Justin bent over the captain's console, straining against the seat harness. "I've brought up sensor displays. When we exit the wormhole you pilot. I'll watch Ferren."

Naomi nodded. "I've programmed in several evasive maneuvers."

"Then we've done all that we can." Justin leaned back in the chair and together they waited.

Justin stared at the chronometer before him and pondered the temporal qualities of the phrase, "anytime now," Then forced his eyes to return to the sensor displays. His slow scan of the console halted over a slowly changing readout. "Ferren is closing on us."

Naomi fastened her seat harness. "I am certain his sensors are better than ours. Most likely we are about to return to normal space."

As if to validate her words, the sensors detected the wormhole event horizon. Stars appeared to break out from a central luminous mass and slide to various positions. Light flashed as Justin attempted to speak. The words choked in his mouth. Weightless and disoriented he floated against the harness.

The ship shot from the gate. With a thud gravity forced him deep into the seat.

Justin squinted at the screen. "What is that?"

The collision alarm sounded.

## Chapter 13

Justin's eyes widened as waves of wreckage swept past.

Naomi swung Surfeit hard to starboard as the aft section of a battleship rolled over them. Turning back to port to avoid other random ship parts of various shapes and sizes, she slid the vessel under the ruined superstructure of another ship.

More alarms sounded. A computer voice reported, "Hull breach, main deck, frame 52. Autosealing."

"We've been hit."

"Ferren?" Naomi shouted over the alarms.

"Hull breach, main deck, frame 47. Autosealing."

Justin silenced the alarms. "No, I don't see him. It's the wreckage. We've flown into a debris field." From the captain's console, he sealed the airtight hatches. Again an alarm sounded. Again, he silenced it. Rubble of all sizes shot past them. "We're getting pummeled by the smaller pieces."

"Too many…too small."

"It's coming from the port side. Try to go with the flow to starboard. Match the speed and direction."

She swung Surfeit starboard.

"Hull breach, main deck, frame 73. Autosealant failure. Reactor coolant failure."

Justin cursed and unclipped his harness.

"Shut down the reactor," Naomi called as she rolled their ship past a huge section of hull.

*I know what to do.* He stood as the ship veered violently. More falling than running, he landed with a thud on the controls. Rolling to the side he lifted the cover and yanked the Scram lever.

The mechanical computer voice declared, "Emergency reactor shutdown complete." Then, with equal calm declared, "Hull breach, Engineering, frame 77. FTL drive failure. Ship on emergency power."

Surfeit swung starboard and Justin, aiming toward the captain's chair, slid, stumbled, then plopped back into it. The arc of a planet now filled the left side of the screen. "Is the debris thinning?"

Naomi veered to avoid a section of hull. "Yes…less now." Seconds later, she fired thrusters and leveled off over the world. She turned away from the helm, breathing like a runner crossing a finish line. Her skin glistened with sweat, "That wreckage, what…where did it come from?"

Justin stood. "I don't know, but I've got to check Mara."

"What do you want me to do?"

As he quickly exited the bridge he said over his shoulder. "Listen for communications from the planet. Try to contact someone." From the passageway he shouted, "If you can't reach anyone, start sensor sweeps."

As he entered his sister's room his eyes locked on an empty bed with sheets half on the floor. "Sis, where are you?"

In the corner, a hand peeked above the bed.

He ran to her.

Ghastly white, Mara sat on the floor against the wall. "What happened?"

He lifted her onto the bed and briefly explained about the orbiting wreckage and damage it did to the ship.

"Seen Titans?"

He shook his head. "No, not yet anyway."

"Leave now," she took a ragged breath, "before they come."

"We can't Sis. We're on emergency power. In a few hours we'll be coasting in a powerless ship and after that…well.…" He let the sentence die.

* * *

No transmission came from the planet, so for the next hour he and Naomi examined sensor logs and new information gathered as they orbited.

"Look here." Justin pointed to the holographic display. "This is the view looking aft just after we exited the gate."

Naomi moved close beside him.

"The display is paused now, but look what happens when I run it forward. See, there's Ferren and…"

"He jumped away." Her face had been somber since they cleared the debris field, but now she gave a weak smile.

"I guess he didn't want to stick around and risk a collision with the rubble but," Justin cleared the display, "I'm sure he'll be back."

"What is all the wreckage?"

"Apparently, it's the remains of a major naval battle. The debris is in a decaying elliptical orbit around the planet. I can identify at least eight Earth Empire ships but, judging from the amount of rubble, I'm certain there were more."

"Were they fighting Titans?"

"I can't be sure, but since Dr. Galen sent you here and the sentinel ship and hologram were Titan, I'd guess that they were involved." She shook her head and mumbled. "Did he really believe Titans would help me?"

Justin knew her question was rhetorical, but he shrugged in response.

Regaining her focus, Naomi scooted her face close to the screen. "What is this distorted patch of space?"

Justin checked. "The sensors don't show anything, so it's probably just an echo." *But it did seem to move with us.*

"Your speculation about Titan involvement coincides with what I have found." She called up a display of the planet. "There were six cities on this world. All sustained significant damage from large-scale nuclear explosions. Radiation levels on the surface vary, but average approximately 200 to 300 rems per year."

"Is that deadly?"

She nodded. "Over time. Also, fallout and dust in the atmosphere appears to have cooled the planet." She pointed to areas in the north and south of the world. "There are glaciers halfway to the equator."

"If Titans lived here they are either dead or gone." He watched her while she stared at the planet below.

She gazed at the displays for a moment. "The Titans are dead and so are we." Slowly her head tilted up and their eyes met. "I'm sorry I led you down this path. You deserve better."

"I have no regrets." It was true, he had no misgivings about meeting her, but he did wish that they were both norms and could have lived a comfortable, ordinary life back in the CFS.

She plopped into a chair. "What should we do?"

"Tell Mara. She deserves to know."

\* \* \*

Sitting together in her room, they explained the situation. "So, it appears there are no Titans here, and the ship is out of fuel and will soon be out of power. I'm sorry Sis. I've run out of ideas."

With a slight nod of her head she whispered, "Skiff."

Justin turned to Naomi. "Can we use it to land on the planet?"

"Yes, there appears to be an intact runway, but as inhospitable as the planet appears it…"

"Is better than here. How long could we live there?"

"The radiation would probably kill us in a month, if the cold does not kill us first."

"One month on the planet looking for a solution or two hours up here. I'll take the former." He kissed his sister on the forehead and hurried from the room.

As they packed what supplies they had into the small craft, Naomi said, "Death up here would be quicker and more peaceful."

"Up here the only possibility is death." He looked out the cockpit window at the world below. "Down there we have options."

"Down there is a one-way trip. We can land, but without fuel we will never take off."

He nodded. "Even if we did take off where would we go?"

"So we are buying only a little time." She stacked the supplies she brought.

"Time to come up with another plan."

"That is the last of the supplies. I'll finish here, you go get Mara."

Justin carried his sister to the skiff and, with Naomi's help, gently laid her on a mat. Using cargo straps, they secured her as best they could.

"Stay here with her. I'll fly us down." Naomi moved to the cockpit.

He strapped himself into a nearby seat. "Hang in there Sis." Reaching out, he took her hand.

She squeezed it as the docking clamps released.

Looking forward, through the cockpit window, the world below seemed soft and white. For several minutes, the ship fell in a quick, but smooth, glide. He watched as the sky slowly turned from black to dark blue. Increasingly the air buffeted the craft until the flames of re-entry engulfed the ship in a fireball falling ever deeper into the atmosphere. A lighter shade of blue greeted them when the fire died away. The craft shot through wispy clouds. Soon the billowy whiteness engulfed the ship. With each moment the air became thicker and more turbulent. Lightning crackled. The tiny skiff shook like a frightened child.

Naomi called over her shoulder, "Did I mention it might be bumpy?"

"No." *This is almost as bad as FTL travel.* He looked down at his sister. Her deathly white skin unnerved him, but her eyes fluttered, assuring him she lived.

Looking forward, white clouds merged seamlessly with the snow-covered ground. The descent smoothed and gradually individual mountains and hills emerged from the whiteness. A fuzzy gray smudge came into view that slowly resolved into a hair-like line. "Is that the runway?"

"Yes."

*Seems narrow.* Moments later, he felt a bump and the screech of the tires. Much to his relief they rolled down the icy smooth landing strip and stopped. The sun was already low on the horizon.

After checking on Mara he joined Naomi in the cockpit. He stared out at the frozen vista. *How does the runway stay clear while snow and ice cover everything else?*

To his right were, in the loosest sense of the word, ten or more buildings. Blackened by fire, windows broken and roofs collapsed, they showed little promise of shelter. He sighed deeply and wondered if landing on the planet had been the right decision. *All I need is one intact hanger.* "How much power do we have?"

"About eight hours."

"Here is my plan. I'm going to go out and...."

She shook her head. "No. Don't you see?" She gestured toward the window then glanced down at the console. "We don't have winter gear and it is -36 degrees."

"It's best I find shelter before nightfall." He stood and moved toward the back.

She followed. "Have you ever been in real cold?"

"Not like this, not freezing cold. Have you?"

She nodded. "We need to find coats, gloves, blankets so you do not kill yourself."

There were no coats, but together they found blankets, wrapped them around his legs, torso and arms, and taped them in place. Justin found a worker's cap that pulled over his ears.

"You look silly, but now you at least you have a chance." She handed him one last blanket. "Hold this over your head and shoulders." Looking him up and down she said, "I wish we had found gloves."

"I'll return as quickly as possible, but I've got to find a place, a hanger maybe, where we can move the ship, find shelter and maybe power." He stepped into the airlock.

"Here." She handed him a light and commlink then reached out and took his hand. "I tried to say something to you on the Titan ship, but…well, I need to say this—just in case." She paused and her countenance filled with determination. "I have loved you since the first time we met."

He smiled at the words he had longed to hear. Stepping close to her, he grasped both her hands and grinned. "The first time we met?"

"Yes."

"That would have been when you swung that steel bar at my head?"

She smiled. "Well, maybe not the very first moment, but not long afterwards."

"I guess you know because of that mind probe thing that I love you too."

Her face flushed as she smiled coyly.

Slowly he moved closer as her eyes fluttered and closed. He wrapped his arms about her and together they stumbled against the control panel.

Raging wind and snow buffeted the two as the outer door slid open. Justin raised his arm against the torrent outside.

Naomi pressed the button to close the door. Brushing snow off, she asked, "Are you sure about this? The storm is awful." Looking out the portal she shivered. "Perhaps it will be better in the morning."

He walked to the portal. The blizzard and the low sun limited visibility. *This may be a nice day on this world.* "By daybreak the skiff will be out of power. We need to find shelter."

He opened the door and stepped out into blowing snow. The feeble light cast a blue hue over the snowy landscape, but he had only an instant to take in the view. Immediately every centimeter of exposed skin numbed. Even his eyes ached as cold wind hit them.

He ran across the runway to a large group of buildings. The first structure had been bombed or burned or both. When he touched the metal wall, cold seemed to scorch his fingers. Coming to an intact building he tried the door. Finding it locked he kicked it in and held up his light, but found a collapsed roof and snow and ice.

In the fading sunlight, he saw a line of hangers ahead, but all were in varying degrees of ruin. Snow swirled out from between the buildings and piled into corners.

One reasonably intact building—that's all I need.

Shadows stirred at the edge of his vision. He wondered if animals or people could be lurking amongst the buildings, but dismissed it all as an illusion of the cold and wind. *I'm probably the only living thing in a thousand kilometers.* The thought numbed him as much as the cold that soaked deep into him.

Unable to move his fingers he turned back toward the ship hoping to warm up and try again. The sun was but a bright spot low in a dark sky. It gave no useful light and would soon drop below the hills. Then the darkness would be total. Intently he looked through the falling snow for the skiff, but could not see it. He walked on, unsure of his direction then stopped as the full realization hit him—he was lost. He reached for the commlink in his pocket, but could hardly hold it in his numb fingers, much less use it. He stumbled, then fell, losing the device in the snow.

His light glowed, just out of reach, through the billowy whiteness. He tried to stand, but the angry wind threw him down. His frozen fingers lost their grip and the blanket flew away. Silent shadows darted at the edge of his light. He crawled for several feet, then stood, stumbled and fell again.

*If I don't get up I'm going to freeze to death.* For several moments, he watched his breath swirl the snow before him. *In a day or two we'll all be dead.* His thoughts drifted to Naomi and the kiss that almost happened just moments ago. The snow swirled over him. *I should have kissed her.* An icy tear rolled down his cheek, but not for him. *I'm sorry Naomi. I'm sorry Mara. I've failed you both.*

Snowflakes knit a shroud that nearly covered him when a feeble shaft of light pierced the darkness. *The ship.* Like a lighthouse beacon, he could follow it home. *Thank you, Naomi.* Painfully he stood and, like a drunk, stumbled toward it. Eyes fixed on the beam he ignored the pain that each step brought. An eternity later, he realized the guiding light came not from Surfeit, but from a window. Two intact hangers stood before him connected by a smaller building. *Whoever they are, I have a better chance with them than out here.* Through the howling wind, he stumbled toward the door. As he neared, it opened and a gust of warm air greeted him.

He stepped forward as five large animals trotted out a doorway. Four legged creatures, covered in black and brown hair, they had long jaws filled with huge carnivorous teeth. Snarling, they moved slowly at the edge of the shadows. Their eyes, reflecting the twilight, looked like red orbs as they moved cautiously into a semi-circle about him. He had seen images of such creatures from Earth. *Wolves.*

He stumbled backward and fell into a snow bank. His eyes locked on the lead beast. One ear stood up and forward, the other hung limp and tattered. A ragged scar ran from its forehead across the face and down to the cheek. From the creature's mind, a single word burst upon Justin's consciousness.

*Stay.*

## Chapter 14

Justin wasn't about to stay. He rolled to his side, leapt to his feet, then stumbled several steps in retreat. Dark figures appeared at the edge of the light. He stopped. *More wolves?* No. These moved on two feet. "Help!"

A light flashed. Electricity shot through his body. Justin convulsed and fell to his knees as darkness engulfed him.

      \*   \*   \*

He was flat on his back. The tips of his fingers, ears, nose and toes tingled, but the rest of him was comfortable and warm. He opened his eyes. Without a move he determined he was on a bed under white sheets. Above him were lights on a white ceiling. Moving just his eyes up and then to the right, he discovered a bare, faded, pink wall. With a slight movement of his head to the left he saw a sink and cabinet in the corner and a small table with three chairs nearby. A closed door stood three meters from his feet. Otherwise the room was bare.

Without a sound, he pulled his arms from under the sheets and examined his carefully bandaged fingers. *Who brought me here?* The thought resounded in his mind. All his life he had a sense of people around him. At a distance, he might not be able to sense their emotions or motives, but he knew they were there, in the next room or down the hall, but now he felt like a man alone in a lifepod drifting in deep space. He glanced around the empty room. *Someone saved my life. Who?* In one quick motion, he threw back the sheets and swung a leg to the floor.

A black wolf, or was it a large dog, trotted around the foot of the bed and eyed him carefully. A tattered ear hung limp and a ragged scar crossed the beast's face.

Justin froze. It was the same animal.

The beast turned and looked at him.

An image flashed through Justin's mind. As if from the animal's eyes, he saw himself sitting on the edge of the bed in his underwear with one foot on the floor. As the image faded from his mind he realized the colors were wrong. The pinkish walls were cool blue and his skin grayish. Again, a single word came to his mind. *Stay.*

The door opened and the animal walked briskly out.

*Wolves? Could this be a race of intelligent wolves?* The idea seemed unlikely. *There were bipeds at the edge of the shadow before.... What had they done?* He remembered a flash of light followed by an electric shock. He looked down at his chest. A red spot remained. *They stunned me.*

Before Justin decided on a course of action the wolf returned. Immediately behind the beast three uniformed men burst into his room with guns drawn.

"Sit down." One of the soldiers scowled and gestured toward the chair with his gun.

"I want to get dressed."

Three red targeting dots appeared on Justin's chest.

The wolf turned and growled at the guards.

Confused, Justin raised his hands. "Okay. Okay." He moved to the chair.

The two silent guards stood several meters to either side, while the one who spoke stationed himself directly behind him. Justin turned to look at those who guarded him, but he could sense only the wolf with his mind, the humans he sensed only with his eyes. It was as if they were holograms and he desperately wanted to reach out and touch them to be reassured that they were real. Glancing from side to side at the guns, he remained seated.

Three or four minutes later two older men, one in a green uniform, the other in blue, entered the room and the soldiers stiffened. Even the wolf stood as if to acknowledge the rank of the pair. From the reaction of the guards and the bearing of the older men, Justin guessed they were officers. *Where have I seen uniforms like that?*

They took seats across from him. The man in blue spoke. "If you attack you will be stunned. Do you understand?"

His accent was strange, but Justin understood him. "Me? Attack you? You attacked me with wolves and stun guns." He pointed to the red mark on his chest.

"They're dogs," Green said turning to look at the animal seated against the far wall. "His name is Thor and none of his pack assaulted you." Fixing his gaze on Justin, he continued. "But one of your friends attacked our people like a berserker."

"Naomi? Is she okay?"

Officer Blue leaned slightly forward. "We need answers and we need them quickly,"

"What about Mara? She was wounded."

Mr. Blue leaned back and stared at him without a word.

"We'd like to answer all your questions," Green said with just the faintest hint of a smile, "but we need answers first."

Justin eyes shot back and forth between them. "What do you want to know?"

"Are you Nephilim?" Green asked.

"Nephilim? Me?" He shook his head. "No. Do I look like some ancient warrior deity?"

"We could ask you questions all day and perhaps, get honest and complete answers," Blue said coolly, "but what we want to do is search your mind."

"You can do that? Are you Titans?"

"We will ask the questions," Mr. Blue said sternly.

"If you can search my mind why don't you just do it?"

Blue started to speak but Green interrupted. "It is a disturbing procedure, sometimes painful. Some call it torture. Our rules do not permit it on civilians without their permission."

Justin recalled how, just before they fled from the microworld, Liberty, Naomi had searched his mind. The process was weird, perhaps unsettling, but not painful or torturous. His eyes drifted between the two men. *Who are these guys and what do they really want to know? Are they Titans? What do I have to hide? What can I hide if they are Titans? They say they want my permission, but do I really have a choice?* He sighed. "Do what you need to do."

"Relax," Green said, "and do not resist."

Within moments, it was as if he had fallen asleep, but he had not. Three minds spun in a whirlpool of thought, spiraling closer, but always deeper into the dark depths of his mind. Fear welled up in him as the last threads of rational thought told him, this was not the technique Naomi had used.

*Relax.*

Like a light that slowly grows brighter, revealing the surrounding terrain, he gradually became aware of two, very disciplined minds searching his memories.

*Why were you on Lepanto?*

*Lepanto?* As he asked the question, the knowledge came to him. The frozen world where they had landed was Lepanto. In that instant the memories of his feeble, frigid, attempt to find refuge flashed through his mind.

The two minds were not interested in those thoughts. *Why were you on Lepanto?*

Like a missile honing in on a target the interrogators raced until Justin found himself crouching at the edge of the docking bay watching his sister and Naomi fight. Anger grew within as he relived the events of that night. Someone grabbed his sister from behind. She head-butted him and Justin fired his gun, killing the man. *No, I didn't kill them, it's just a memory.*

*Relax.*

On the far side of the bay, Naomi performed her dance of death, pirouetting from one man and slamming into another. He saw Ferren moving toward Naomi. He fired his weapon as anger flared red hot within him. He fired repeatedly as he raced toward the man who attacked her. *You're the cause of this!*

Memories that had been lost in the rage now roared to the surface. He emptied his gun and threw it aside. He ran toward Ferren, intending to choke the life out of him. Coming near, Justin thrust his arm toward the pirate's throat. The fat man struggled to breath and flailed at his neck. Justin slowly, but effortlessly, moved his arm higher. The pirate kicked vainly as he lifted into the air. But, Justin never touched him, he had done it all with his mind.

The memory of Ferren hanging in the air froze, reversed, raced forward and back as the minds of Mr. Blue and Green lingered in the background like fascinated mental voyeurs.

One of the minds smiled with a thought. *Some of our vanguard did survive.*

The other mind was less impressed. *The Nephilim have fooled us before. The mind refocused on him. If you are Titan, what is your rank and genome designation?*

With laser-like precision, his interrogators target the needed memories which came back vivid and clear. Once again he stood on the bridge of the ancient Titan ship.

The sentinel announced, "There is another person on the bridge. Come forward and be identified."

He placed his hand in the outline. "Ouch." The prick of the finger stung just as it did then. He looked at his finger. Was it real or was this a memory? A single drop of blood formed and his DNA sequence scrolled on the ancient ship's screen.

The two minds fixed on the last line of the display, genome designation: 133-37. Specialty: Naval Line Officer.

From his interrogators Justin sensed a mixture of emotions: confusion, wonder, and from one mind, a sense of awe. *Who are your parents?*

*No! Not there. Not that memory. I won't.* But he did and watched his mother die again.

## Chapter 15

Justin opened his eyes. Canine teeth and warm breath greeted him. Mouth hanging open, Thor stood beside him. Frightened and realizing he was on his floor, Justin flailed his arms, striking the dog on the snout.

The beast yelped.

Heart racing, he struggled to his feet as the dog silently stepped back.

A voice came from one side. "Thor will not harm you." A silver-haired man with a close-cropped beard patted pressed, and folded, items on the table beside him. "Here are your clothes."

Justin stumbled and fell against the wall as he rose. "Who are you?"

As the dog retreated to the far side of the room, the man spoke. "My name is Leo. Are you hungry? Get dressed and I'll explain what I can over breakfast."

Justin stared at the old man in civilian clothes for a moment then walked to the basin and splashed water on his face. "Where are the two who interrogated me? I…we have unfinished business." The emotions of the relived events remained vivid and raw in his mind. He wanted to strangle the two, just as he had Ferren, but thought better of actually saying it.

"They will not disturb you again."

"What does that mean?"

"They are recovering from the ordeal of your interrogation."

Justin shot the man an angry glance. "Yeah, so am I."

The older man nodded. "But you have had a lifetime to deal with your actions and the resulting feelings."

He shook his head slowly and tried to bury the resurrected memories.

"For them it is as if just yesterday their mother died, they were abandoned, enslaved, struggled to survive, and killed people." He held up an antique slate. "I read the report while I waited for you to wake."

Justin stared at him trying to understand. "They feel everything from my life as if it happened to them just yesterday?"

The old man nodded. "For them it all *did* happen yesterday."

It was hard for Justin to feel empathy for his interrogators, but they had paid a price for what they had done to him. He had spent a lifetime building dark corners in his mind that he rarely visited. He sighed and no longer wished to add to their pain.

"We will watch them for a time to ensure they do no harm to themselves."

Putting on his shirt, he pushed the grilling from his mind. He turned and faced Leo. "Who are you? Where is Naomi? Is Mara okay?"

"Mara is recovering. Naomi is well and the people looking after her are fine—as long as they keep their distance."

Justin grinned as he remembered his own first moments struggling with Naomi. "Where are they? I want to see them." He paused. "Where am I?"

Leo motioned for him to follow. "I need some breakfast."

"I need some answers," he growled.

Standing at the door, the older man looked back at Justin with a grin. "And you shall have them, but patience is a virtue."

Answers would only come, Justin realized, when Leo was willing to give them and that appeared to be during breakfast.

Frustrated, he followed the older man out the door with the dog close behind. They stepped into a large, well equipped, but nearly empty, medical ward. The gleaming pastel walls, polished floors, and shining equipment, seemed to announce the care of the staff.

Justin turned and smiled at a young, very pregnant, woman. She smiled back and returned to caring for one of the few patients. The two men continued down the length of the room toward large double doors. Only as they neared the exit did he realize he had sensed the woman's presence before turning to see her. While ahead of him, leading the way out, Leo remained a blank slate, like a holographic image.

Desperately he wanted to know who these people were. The two interrogators, with their incredible mental powers, seemed to be Titans, but Leo's mind didn't register with Justin at all. *How would I phrase it? "I'm curious, are all of you the criminal traitors who committed genocide against the human race? Just wondering."*

Leo looked over his shoulder with a quizzical grin at Justin. The doors before him opened and he stepped through.

As Justin exited, he decided just to ask. "Are you a Ti...?" He stopped and stared out the window before him. Slowly he stepped forward. The arch of a giant microworld stretched out in the dim morning light before him. From his left the great oval rose high above. There, hanging over him, were great bodies of water, farms and forests. Then on his right the arc continued down until it disappeared beyond a hill. He looked straight ahead trying to gauge the length of the vessel. The far end disappeared in the mist. Obviously, it was many times larger than Liberty, the microworld he had so recently fled. *I'm not on that frozen planet, Lepanto.*

Leo stood beside him. "An engineer friend of mine once described this ship as a world on the inside of a tin can," He pointed to vast fields and forests that appeared to hang down from the surface several kilometers above, "but I think that minimizes the beauty of it."

Far above, banks of huge lights were just coming on, simulating dawn. Justin shook his head slowly. He had heard stories of vessels constructed on such a scale for the Nephilim, but they were part temple, part warship. This mammoth vessel appeared to be a complete ecosystem and at least one city, all hanging in an arch before him. Justin turned toward Leo his mouth agape. "Terra Nova? Is this the microworld Terra Nova?"

"Not what I would call micro, but yes it is—or rather was."

"But at the end of Titanomachy War, the Titans destroyed it during the Battle for Earth."

"Is that what your history books tell you?" He turned and strolled toward the building exit.

With eyes on the vista beyond the glass, Justin followed. Several dozen people lingered in the lobby. With his gaze only occasionally darting from the window, he hardly noticed the people glancing in his direction.

As they stepped out of the building, Leo continued. "We rechristened the ship and gave it the name Exodus because...."

"You took the ship—why?" Justin hurried to catch up.

"We needed it." Leo shook his head. "Why would we destroy such an impressive unarmed vessel?"

*Because you're Titans, and you were designed to kill or destroy everything in your path.* But, the old man didn't seem like a killer so Justin held his tongue and simply shrugged.

Leo led him down along a broad sidewalk with the dog close behind.

At the sound of splashing, Justin looked over the rail and discovered a stream following the walkway on their right. Water dashed over and around rocks on the way toward the plaza just ahead. He looked back up the gentle slope behind them, but couldn't decide which of the several large buildings on, or near the top they had exited.

The older man followed his gaze. "That is the hospital complex." He pointed. "You were in the smaller clinic just to the left." Turning, he gestured. "Just ahead, in the plaza, there is an excellent little restaurant that overlooks what we call Sunrise Park."

The dawn grew brighter as they walked. Justin glanced up at the massive banks of lights high above. "Why do you call it Sunrise Park?"

"Because many of us start the day there."

Leo walked to a table as they entered the square, but Justin went to the rail that overlooked the commons. With the dog seated beside him, he took in the vista. The stream flowed along one side into a reservoir about one hundred meters away.

In front of him, and just below, a large grassy field filled with people. Formations of men and women in sweaty, athletic gear jogged into the park then lined up. *Those in the military formations were probably Titans, but others mingled at the edges? Civilians? Families?*

Justin watched the growing crowd. Three groups formed to his left. Justin moved in that direction, but bumped into the dog. "Ah, excuse me. I, ah want to...."

Thor moved out of his way.

"Thanks." He followed the railing to a better position.

Two men, each holding a flag, trotted to positions near the center front of the formation. No breeze stirred, but the flags fluttered as the men trotted into position. One flag was inscribed with a number, 33, while the other bore a fish symbol like the one etched in Naomi's medallion and on the uniform of the officer in his painting back in what had been his home.

A man in a neat green uniform and gray hair at his temples took a position in front of the middle unit. The uniform was like that of his interrogators and Justin assumed he must be an officer.

Slowly the man scanned along the men and women before him. "Platoon sergeants, report!"

One of the sergeants saluted. "Sir, first platoon is present and accounted for." In turn, the other two sergeants reported.

After the reports, the officer gave the plan of the day and then slowly scanned the men. "Okay Marines, when you're dismissed form up along the service road for physical training. Platoon sergeants dismiss your men."

As the platoons moved out a young man ran up to one of the sergeants standing almost immediately below Justin.

"Sarge, what about the rumors of strangers on...."

"Haven't I told you jarheads not to listen to rumors?"

"But Sarge, the prophecy."

"No news is true unless, or until, I tell you it's true." He looked back over the group. "Come on, get a move on."

Back in the CFS, Justin had visited a few military installations as part of his business and seen similar morning gatherings. *If they are Titans, they seem very normal—in a military kind of way.*

"The food is getting cold."

Justin turned at the sound of Leo's voice. The older man sat at a table with two breakfast plates not three meters away. "Go ahead. I'll be right there." He returned his gaze to the park below as a man about his age walked into the plaza carrying a child and holding the hand of a woman. With the woman at the soldier's side Justin could not see his uniform, but something about it drew his attention. The couple strolled into the empty space left when the previous unit departed. Just below him they stopped. The man kissed the child then handed the infant to the woman. Still holding her hand, the man spoke to her, but the words were lost in the noise of the plaza. Then he kissed her and jogged off toward one of the other formations. It was as the man hurried away that Justin saw his uniform. The soldier was a shadow warrior, the elite shock troops of the Titan.

Cold fear gripped him.

Thor whined and rubbed his head against Justin's leg.

Taking a deep breath he found the mother and child in the crowd below. Anywhere else and he might have assumed, from there casual affection, that they were a family. *Shadow Warriors have feelings? Titans have families and children? Perhaps the Titans have changed over the centuries.* He sighed and a smile spread slowly across his face. Images of Naomi and Mara flashed through his mind. *Perhaps, just perhaps, we have found a refuge.* He turned to speak to Leo. "Oh, the food."

Leo looked up from his mostly empty plate and, with mouth full, motioned for Justin to join him at the table.

Justin stepped from the rail and immediately caught the eye of a passerby staring in his direction. The man turned away but, as Justin sat, he noticed another person watching him. Once again, he quickly turned away. Then as a woman walked by, she turned and, just for a moment, their eyes locked.

Leo pushed his plate away. "What did you want to ask me?"

Justin's eyes darted about the plaza. Even the dog stared at him. *Why is everyone looking at me?*

## Chapter 16

Leo smiled as he leaned back in his chair. "Everyone is looking at you because you broadcast your every thought to them."

Justin stared at the older man. Nothing emanated from him. He looked at the people in the plaza, some of whom still stared in his direction, but he could only sense them with his eyes. *I sure would like to learn how to hide my thoughts.* He fixed his eyes on Leo. *I've wondered how to ask this and now appears to be a good time and this seems a good way—are you a Titan?"*

Leo seemed about to laugh. "Yes. Most of us are."

"Most?"

"There are some Norms with us."

Justin tapped his fork on the table as he recalled the pregnant woman he had sensed on the hospital ward. "Why would Norms willingly go with Titans?"

"Even during wars, people fall in love."

He studied the face of the older man. Leo had an easy smile and although Justin tried to remain skeptical, it was difficult. The smell of the food diverted his attention. Hunger got the best of him. He reached for the fork and took the first bite of his breakfast. "The war was a long time ago...." The elder seemed about to speak, but he was impatient to ask his questions. "Why did your people turn on normal humans and attack Earth?"

"They are your people also."

Justin reluctantly nodded. The evidence that he was a Titan appeared insurmountable. His eyes drifted to the plate of food. It looked like scrambled eggs, pancakes, butter and syrup, but it tasted better. He remembered the factory back on liberty that produced all sorts of dry, cracker-like food. It kept him alive for years until he could afford real food—occasionally.

The elder continued. "Before I share our history, tell me what the Norms say of those events."

"The Titan soldiers turned against normal humans."

"Why?"

"The Alien War was over, but the Titans didn't return for decommissioning. They didn't obey the orders of Earth."

Leo slowly shook his head. "So, what did the Titans supposedly do?"

Chewing on another bite he said, "They waged war against their creators."

"Creators? They teach you that normal humans created us?"

"Of course you...we...were created. The Project Titan creators gave us our strength, our mental powers?"

"We're naturally fit and most of us work to stay that way, but we're not superhuman. As for the mental abilities, no one knows for sure, but when the original Titans departed Earth, they left as normal humans."

Justin shook his head.

"Project Titan selected intelligent, genetically healthy and athletic humans, the best and brightest, to fight the alien threat. Our ancestors left, in a fleet of sub-light ships, for the endangered colonies."

Justin nodded. Except for the part about sending normal humans, Leo was repeating Norm history. "But the mental powers?"

Leo shrugged. "Some think they are the result of random mutation, others say it is a miracle, a gift from God or the prophet. What we do know is that our ancestors, the early Titans, left Earth more than a century before these abilities began to appear."

Justin frowned skeptically.

"However it happened, those capabilities slowly spread through the population so that we now all have them, to varying degrees."

"So, after the Alien War, the Titans just *decided* to wage a war of genocide against their human brothers?" Justin asked sarcastically.

"Genocide? That's what you've been taught?" Leo rubbed his head. "Tell me the rest. What do they teach you about the Battle of Earth?"

"After defeating the main Norm fleet, they continued and attacked the remaining forces over Earth. The Titans bombarded the planet, hitting every continent."

"Does history tell you who led the attack on Earth?"

"Fleet Admiral Leonidas."

The old man nodded and seemed to age in an instant. "Yes, the historians got that right. It was my responsibility."

"Your responsibility? That was four hundred years ago. How could it be…."

"As they say, time is relative."

Justin's eyes narrowed.

"Have you studied time dilation?" He tilted his head. "What happens to a ship traveling at a significant fraction of light speed?"

"Time slows down for those on the vessel."

"After capturing Terra Nova and making a couple of short FTL jumps we have been accelerating at sub-light speed for nearly twenty years as we measure time. Apparently about four hundred years have passed from your perspective. Relative to you, time for us has slowed to a crawl."

"Are you saying….?"

"Four hundred years ago as you measure time, I led the Titan forces in their attack on Earth and the capture of Terra Nova. I am Fleet Admiral Leonidas."

Justin's words came slowly and almost at a whisper. "Millions died in the battle and nearly a billion in the civil war and the famine that followed."

The old man's eyes dimmed and he nodded slowly. "I knew that many…many died and I feared that even more would die in the chaos that would surely come, but we had to go."

He didn't understand what Leonidas meant about having to go, but Justin wanted to go, to run somewhere—anywhere. Since he had discovered what he was, he'd hoped that, over the centuries, the Titans had changed. No nation, no group, were the same after so much time, but for these people it had not been so long. They had lived—had fought, the Battle of Earth. They were the creatures who had turned against their human brothers and slaughtered them in a series of attacks leading up to the decisive battle. It was only there, high over Earth, that the Titan fleet had been defeated with, as many claimed, the help of the Nephilim. All that devastation and death had led to civil war and famine. Historical images ran through his mind of burning cities, dead bodies, and the walking skeletons of the survivors.

Anguish swept from Leonidas. With eyes closed he held out his hand as if to stop Justin's thoughts.

Those nearby turned their heads toward them. Some stood and moved closer.

Others moved away.

Justin stood and ran.

\* \* \*

Justin heard a dog trot toward the table in a quiet corner of a park where he had sought refuge. As the animal approached he glanced to his right to ensure it was Thor. "So, you found me," he said with little emotion.

The dog seemed to smile as it sat beside him with its tongue flopped out to the side.

Moments later Fleet Admiral Leonidas, the worst war criminal in human history, walked up, carrying a tray. "I brought you another breakfast."

"Thanks," he said flatly and motioned for him to set it down.

"You realize that it's impossible to hide from us until you learn to conceal your thoughts."

Justin had figured that out an hour earlier. He had sat at a table and attempted to sort through all he had been told while waiting for someone to approach and…. He wasn't sure what might happen.

"Would you like me to show you how to do that?"

Huh?

Teach you how to hide your thoughts.

*Sure.* He motioned for the old man to sit down. As he did their eyes locked. *How could I be a Titan?* The thought had just occurred to him.

Leonidas shot him a questioning glance.

He hadn't meant to ask the question, but in this place his every thought was part of the conversation. "If all of you have been on this ship for four hundred years, how am I a Titan?"

"It's not just this ship, we have a fleet, but we needed Exodus to carry the bulk of our marines."

He nodded, but was still confused.

Leonidas took a deep breath. "Once, years ago, I had a wife and four sons." He paused and his eyes became very distant. "Only one survived the wars. Simon was young and ambitious, eager to prove himself."

Justin pecked at his food as the old man again paused.

"After capturing Terra Nova and jumping away from Earth we sent a vanguard mission to Lepanto. Simon volunteered to go."

"They never came back?"

The old man shook his head. "I thought it was safer than staying with the main fleet, so I was glad to see him go, but engine problems onboard Exodus caused us to miss the rendezvous. We couldn't contact them after that." The life seemed to drain from the older man's face. "I feared all were dead."

Justin put down his fork. "But they didn't die. There were several cities on Lepanto." Memories of the wrecked ships and a planet engulfed in a nuclear winter leapt to his mind. *A battle.*

Leonidas nodded. "Apparently many years later, as you measure time, the Titans on Lepanto were discovered by the Empire but," he paused, "we found very few bodies in the rubble and only one ship with Titan markings."

"They escaped?"

Again, the old man smiled. "We believe so—hope so. They had warning."

He leaned forward. "Warning? How?" *And how would you know?*

"The Prophecies of Justin warned us." Leonidas pulled a small book from his jacket pocket. "Our children memorize it in school." He set the book on the table. "Justin brought us the message of a loving God."

"Titans believe this?"

His face still serious, the older man gave a hint of a smile and nodded. "Your parents probably named you after him."

Justin shook his head.

"His message spread slowly at first. I didn't believe until the normal humans turned against us." He tapped the book. "Justin foretold it."

It was then he remembered his original question. *How am I related to all of them? How can I be a Titan if all of you have been traveling for hundreds of years?* For several moments he tried to put the pieces of information together. "So I am...?"

"A survivor from Lepanto."

## Chapter 17

Justin picked up his fork and played with his food. He didn't believe in prophets or messages from God, but the missing pieces of his life seemed to be falling into place. He was a Titan and his family had lived on Lepanto until someone, probably Earth Empire, attacked the planet. Childhood memories of alarm bells and the rumble of distant explosions raced through his mind. He had closed the hatch on his mother during the attack. He had killed her. Probably, his father had also died that day. His mouth felt dry. An old thirst had returned. He stabbed at the food. *What next?*

"You and your friends are Titans and the only known descendants of our vanguard. It is my hope...our hope, that you will choose to remain here, but we will not force you."

Justin's eyes locked on Leonidas. "So, if I...we, my friends, choose, we are free to go?"

"I don't believe you have a means to leave at the moment, but when you do, yes you are free."

He recalled Naomi's stated willingness to kill Titans and Mara's attempted suicide when she realized she was one. They would not want to remain. He sighed. "We may never have the means to leave." *Even if we all wanted to.*

"I've asked technicians at our space dock orbiting Lepanto to repair your vessel." He smiled weakly. "Even an old admiral has some influence."

"Really? When will it be ready? We can help."

"I'm afraid your ship is of low priority, but it should be ready when we get to the system in just over a week."

"A week? Why so long to get there?"

"Remember, we are traveling at sub-light speed."

"But Terra Nova was an FTL vessel, the biggest one ever built."

Leonidas nodded. "*Was* is the key word in your sentence. Earth forces hit the ship several times during the battle, damaging the FTL engines. They failed after a few short jumps. We've been trying to fix them for years. Our repair dock is attempting to salvage the needed parts from the many destroyed ships still in orbit around the planet."

Justin eyes drifted down to the table as he allowed all he had heard to sink in. Finally, he lifted his gaze. "It seems that I have a week to get to know you before I make a decision."

The faintest hint of a smile crossed the old man's face. "That is all I hoped for—right now."

Justin leaned forward. "Where are my friends? We have a lot to talk about."

\* \* \*

Justin cautiously opened the hatch wondering how he might be received. A chair crashed into the wall beside his head and exploded into fragments. Instinctively he dove behind the door.

"Get out or die!"

From behind the door he called out, "Naomi it's me, Justin."

Silence. Then a sheepish voice, "Really? Justin is it you?"

"Yes. I'm going to open the door and…"

The hatch flew from his hand and Naomi swept him into her arms. "They said you were alive, but…I didn't know if…." She kissed him. "You should have told me." With her arms still around him, they stumbled back into the room. Her eyes locked on him. *You could have—should have—contacted me this way.*

*They taught me techniques they said would keep my thoughts private, but I couldn't be sure. You were the test.*

Confusion clouded her face.

*If I could get close, without you knowing, then I would know my thoughts were private.*

Minutes slipped by as they sat beside one another holding hands. Only occasionally a sound escaped their lips as Justin described the light that he thought was the ship, the pack of telepathic dogs and being stunned.

Naomi nodded. *When I couldn't contact you, I dressed as best I could against the cold and opened the hatch. They were waiting for me. We fought. I think I hurt one or two, but they had the advantage of both surprise and some form of stun weapon. I awoke here.*

*Have they treated you well?*

*Yes, I guess, but when they told me they were Titans I...* Her eyes darted about the spartanly furnished room and rested first on a busted table in the corner and then on the shattered chair by the door. *I broke off contact.* She giggled.

Justin smiled then told of awakening in a space place and the mind probe interrogation. Finally, he described meeting Leonidas, discovering that he was on Terra Nova, and the older man's admission that he led the Titan fleet in the Battle of Earth. Naomi was familiar with time dilation, but it still took several minutes to explain that the people who rescued them were the Titans of the Titanomachy War and the Battle of Earth.

Justin tried to explain how his own feelings had evolved over the last two days as they continued to talk. Finally he sighed. *I guess what I'm trying to say is after they knew that I wasn't an enemy, that I was a Titan, they treated me well.* He held up his hand showing the several fingers still bandaged due to frostbite. *I've walked all over Exodus....*

Naomi didn't understand and let Justin feel her puzzlement.

*Terra Nova. They changed the name of the ship after they captured it at the Battle of Earth.*

*You sound like you want to stay here.*

*We are Titans.*

*But these are the people who attacked Earth. The war they waged destroyed the United Planets and allowed the Nephilim to take control. How can we stay?*

Justin stood and looked about the compartment. *We don't have to stay here. Well, as long as you promise not to hurt anyone.*

She nodded. *I promise, as long as I am with you and they stay back.*

He smiled. That was probably the best he could hope for now. *Then let's go back to Exodus.* They stood. *We'll see Mara.* Justin stepped toward the door then paused and turned. "And dinner tonight will be a bit of a surprise. Try to keep an open mind. Okay?"

"Okay," she said hesitantly. As they walked to the door she asked, "What took you so long to get here?"

"Actually it was you that came to me."

"Huh?"

He gave her a quick grin. "Because of our injuries, they rushed Mara and me back to the main fleet where they had hospital facilities, but they kept you on a ship in the Lepanto system. Shortly after they discovered we were Titans I asked to see you. They rotated your ship back to the main fleet as soon as they could." Stepping out the door he said, "I came here as soon as you arrived."

She smiled at him.

"And when I got here you threw a chair at me."

She thumped his chest. "I didn't know..."

He laughed, as they walked down the passageway hand-in-hand.

\* \* \*

Justin and Naomi packed into a shuttle with people who had completed a week of duty in and around Lepanto. The two found a seat near a portal on the crowded shuttle, and after it launched took in the vista of other vessels heading toward a giant microworld.

That's our destination, Exodus or Terra Nova," Justin said.

Throngs of people swarmed about them as several shuttles emptied into the Exodus docking port. Walking across the platform Justin said. "Yesterday morning, after I finished what Leonidas called, 'primary school mental training,' he offered to get someone to show me around."

Naomi's eyes narrowed. "A spy."

"I thought of that, so I told him I already had someone in mind."

"Oh, who is it?"

Up ahead in the crowd a pregnant woman waved.

"Her," he said waving back. "I think you'll like Becca; she's a norm." He said as he walked towards her.

"Why would that make me like her?"

*You can read her thoughts. It's against all Titan rules of decorum, but I wanted to know if she had been told to hide anything from me.*

*Was she?*

*No.* As they approached, Justin introduced the two women.

"You made a pregnant woman show you around?" Naomi said.

"I was glad to do it."

Smiling at his guide, Justin said, "You didn't have to come here. I could have...."

She shook her head and smiled. "No, that's not why I'm here. My husband is coming on another shuttle."

"Glad to hear it," Justin said. Looking back and forth between the women he asked, "Should we wait and meet your husband?"

"No. He will be stuck here with his platoon for a while and I know you want to see Mara. Go ahead and, if she is well enough, bring her to dinner tonight."

"Dinner?" Naomi said with some surprise. "Perhaps we should not. Your husband is…"

"It's fine. He wanted to meet all of you and," she patted her stomach, "cooking is about all I can do now."

As they walked away from Becca, Naomi shot Justin a glance. *I sensed the baby's mind reaching out to us. Is her husband a Titan?*

*Yes.*

*We are eating with one of them?*

Justin shook his head. *Is it possible that much of what they taught you in the Empire is a lie?*

*From what you have told me, they do not deny the worst of what we both have been taught.*

*Just try to keep an open mind.*

She stopped and took his arm. "Try to remain skeptical."

"They did save us on Lepanto and in a few days we will know if they have repaired our ship."

"And if they let us, we should leave."

"They've been kind and apparently honest."

"Don't forget, they are genetically enhanced killers."

The last moments of Garrett's life flashed through Justin's mind. "They deny being genetically enhanced and whatever they are, so are we."

"We are not killers and we are hundreds of years removed from them. We may be their descendants, but these are the creatures that killed hundreds of millions."

Justin nodded. Leonidas, and others, had admitted their guilt, but for hardened mass-murderers, they seemed strangely troubled by the events.

She took his arm and pulled him in close. "I could never stay with these people."

He sighed. "Okay, when Surfeit is ready, we'll collect Mara and leave."

Alarms sounded.

## Chapter 18

"General quarters, general quarters, all hands man your battle stations." The message seemed to come from everywhere.

Justin's eyes flashed right and left as the crowd hurried in all directions. He looked for his guide, Becca, but she was already lost in the multitude that now flowed toward every exit. Turning to Naomi he asked, "Do you think it's a drill?"

Naomi, still holding him by the arm, shook her head. "Were they listening? Did they hear our plan to leave?"

"Bring an entire ship to battle stations because *we* want to leave?"

A stubborn expression covered her face and, with a shrug she asked, "What's your plan? What should we do?"

He cursed the alarm as he tried to think. "Let's go to Mara."

Even as they hurried from the docking platform, people shut some of the hatches and locked them down. With Justin in the lead they joined others heading down a wide passageway toward the central core of Exodus.

Entering the open expanse of the habitat, Naomi slowed then stopped. "It is huge—and beautiful." The crowd attempted to flow around, but some jostled her as they passed.

Justin followed her eyes as they drifted along the arc of the ship and the buildings, farms, lakes and rivers that seemed to hang from the sky. After a few seconds he stepped toward her. "Yes, lovely." He took her hand, "but let's keep moving."

Within minutes, they trotted up the walkway that, just two days before, he and Leonidas had casually walked down. Few people were visible as they reached the top of the hill.

The alarm stopped as thy neared the clinic door and, the voice from everywhere announced, "Condition one, set throughout the ship."

"Condition one? What does that mean?" he asked rhetorically. The clinic door slid open.

"The ship is ready for battle," Naomi said following him in.

"How do you know that? Where you in the navy?" Justin picked up speed.

"I was trained as a Marine."

Justin raced around the final corner to Mara's room. Two armed men came down the hall. He stopped abruptly.

"Are you Justin, Justin Garrett?" one of them asked.

Naomi turned the corner and slammed into his back.

A third man pushed Mara in a wheelchair out of the room.

Justin smiled at his sister. "How are you doing?"

She smiled weakly. "Getting better."

The other man repeated his question. "Are you Justin Garrett?"

Naomi stepped forward. *What do they want? Where are they taking Mara?*

Justin felt her fear.

Her eyes darted between him and the marines. *When they get closer, we could take them.*

Out the door came Thor, his tongue hanging to the side. The dog seemed to smile and that reassured Justin. He took Naomi's hand and held tight. *And after we 'take them' then what?* "Yes, I'm Justin."

"Fleet Admiral Leonidas requests you follow us to combat." The two-armed men moved past Justin and Naomi and disappeared around the corner. As Mara rolled by, Justin noticed the medic insignia on the sleeve of the man pushing her. Momentarily, he touched his sister's hand, then turned to follow.

Mara looked over her shoulder and smiled at him again. He knew she was pleased to see him, but it wasn't the smile that told him so. Even with his minimal training, he now sensed her emotions and thoughts and knew she felt nothing radiating from him. He mused how much things had changed in just a couple of days. Out of politeness, he blocked out her mind.

As they exited, a breathless Becca came toward the clinic. When her eyes rested on Mara in the wheelchair, she held up her arm, "Stop."

Everyone halted.

Becca bent over and breathed deeply. "Where…are you…taking…my patient?"

The soldiers quickly explained their orders and the medic then discussed Mara's condition and care with Becca.

Justin grinned that armed Titan soldiers stopped and explained themselves to a winded, pregnant normal human.

"Okay, if you feel up to it Mara, but," Becca turned to the medic, "you get her back here as soon as we secure from general quarters."

The group moved on as Becca continued to the clinic. Thor lead, followed by the two-armed marines. Mara and the medic came next. Everyone moved quickly behind the trotting dog.

Justin followed the others pondering how Thor seemed to know where they were going. Naomi jogged to his side and he locked eyes with her. *They said, Leonidas 'wants us to follow them to combat?' I don't hear any shooting, any combat. What do you think they meant?*

Naomi smiled at him. *Military vessels navigate from the Bridge, but they fight from the Combat Center. For some reason the admiral wants us there.*

\*     \*     \*

Justin had visited the farms and communities that made up the core of Exodus, but now, with his friends, he followed the marines into the superstructure. This part of the vessel looked like the interior of a ship, gray and austere. They passed through several airtight doors. When he rounded a corner, Justin saw two marines standing on either side of a large, airtight hatch. As they approached, one of the guards opened the door and stood aside.

Once within, their armed escort reported to the admiral and then departed, but the medic and Thor remained nearby. The compartment was roughly square with displays and consoles along the bulkheads and down the middle of most of it. The wall farthest from them presented a digital display of a solar system. Immediately in front of it was a large holographic map of part of the system. Justin could see a star, several planets and comets along with a host of nearby vessels. Leonidas moved with several other officers toward the holo display.

Justin looked down at Mara in her chair, took her hand and gave it a gentle squeeze. Leaning down he whispered, "I came to see you the last two days, but you were always asleep."

"They told me. I'm sorry I missed you."

A tiny red light flashed on the wheelchair. For the first time Justin noticed a tube from the chair to Mara's arm. The medic came up and made adjustments and the light went out.

Naomi moved closer and with a tilt of her head directed his attention back to the display. In a low voice she said, "The bulk of the Titan fleet is in the Lepanto system Kuiper belt."

Wondering why that was significant, he whispered agreement.

"But, see those two red dots? Those are unidentified ships."

As she spoke, the display zoomed in on the area around the frozen planet of Lepanto. Leonidas gestured toward two trajectory lines arching from the jump gate. Justin nodded. Apparently, two ships entered the system using the gate. Immediately upon exiting, the two vessels veered away from the debris field and were now on an arching course toward the yellow star at the center of the system. He fixed his gaze on Naomi. *I guess we caused similar excitement when we arrived.*

Naomi smiled.

Justin's eyes drifted to his left past a dozen men and women staring at consoles until they settled upon an older man standing alone at the far end of the compartment. *Mr. Green.* He fought to contain the thoughts and the emotions the erupted with seeing one of his interrogators from a couple of days ago.

Green nodded to Justin, and then turned to the Admiral. "The captain of the lead vessel has ordered a search of the system."

Leonidas kept his eyes on the holographic display. "What are they looking for?"

Green's eyes closed and his head drifted down. Seconds passed then, with eyes still closed, he spoke. "His orders are to retrieve three fugitives. Two are wanted as Titans."

It felt to Justin like every eye fixed on him and his companions.

Admiral Leonidas turned from the display and for the first time acknowledged the presence of Justin and the others. With a motion of his arm, he invited them to approach the holo display. "Our ship database is four centuries out of date. Can you tell us anything about these vessels?" The admiral nodded to a technician and the detailed image of two ships appeared before them.

Instantly Justin recognized one of the vessels. "The smaller one is the Acheron, a pirate ship."

"Pirate ship?" Leonidas repeated with surprise in his voice.

Mara leaned forward for a better look and then groaned. "Ferren? He's still following us?"

"It is worse than that," Naomi added, "The larger ship is an imperial reconnaissance vessel."

Leonidas sighed. "What weapons do they have?"

Justin described the Acheron missile launchers and lasers. "I don't know what the imperial ship has." Everyone in the group turned to Naomi.

"I hate the Nephilim, but I am a loyal citizen of the Empire, a soldier. I will not tell you how to destroy an imperial ship."

Leonidas frowned. "You're a Titan and the Nephilim are hunting for you. I strongly suspect they will kill you if you fall into their hands."

"I am not a Titan. I am a clone. I was created to...." Her voice trailed off into silence.

The admiral looked at her incredulously. Then the word came slowly from his mouth, "Clone?" He shot a questioning glance at the medic who shook his head. "Talk to him about the details. You're not a clone," he waved his hand between Naomi and Mara, "but you two *are* sisters."

## Chapter 19

Naomi backed away. "Sisters?"

Justin shook his head in disbelief. From Mara came a wave of surprise. He turned to her, but she stared at Naomi.

"We don't have time for your misplaced loyalties," the admiral said flatly.

Justin needed no telepathic abilities to see the anger of Leonidas, as the Admiral stared at Naomi with cold eyes.

"The recon ship will soon discover us," he continued. "Will you help us?"

Naomi shook her head.

The admiral's eyes shot to Mr. Green. Justin followed his gaze in time to see Green's brow rise slightly. Apparently, the two officers were communicating telepathically.

With a shake of his head, the admiral seemed to reject whatever they were discussing. He turned to a technician. "Get Admiral Cottrell on the command ship."

A holographic image appeared in an open space near the center of the compartment. A gray-haired man, perhaps a little younger than Leonidas, appeared. Seated, the man swiveled to the side. "What can I do for you, Leo?"

"I have some intel for you Admiral." Leonidas approached the projected image and described the weapons of the pirate ship and his lack of knowledge regarding the recon vessel, but without mentioning Naomi or her refusal to help.

Cottrell leaned back in his chair. "We can destroy them both, but when they don't return others will follow." He rubbed his chin. "Any chance of getting the Exodus FTL engines online?"

"Not before we're discovered. The engines we pulled from the debris field need a human interface. We're still trying to reverse engineer it."

Cottrell nodded. "I'll have the Excalibur battle group move to your flank and release weapons. When they fire on us, we fire on them."

Leonidas nodded as the image dissolved.

Justin noticed lights turn red on a nearby console. A technician announced, "Weapons free."

Naomi moved up against the bulkhead and seemed to try to blend in. Justin ambled in her general direction. He wanted to talk to her, maybe comfort her, but he didn't know if he'd be welcomed so he stopped several meters away. Together with the fleet, they waited.

Sometime later Leonidas approached. "Have you ever been in battle?"

"No," Justin said to the older man, "but I've been shot at."

The admiral smiled, nodded, then turned his attention to the holo display a few meters away.

All of his life, Justin had quickly been able to determine the nature of the person before him. He studied the admiral's face. History labeled him a mass murderer, but all he had seen was a thoughtful, caring person. Was this all a mask covering a darker side that he was unable to see? He wondered if he would ever know the truth of the man. They watched the display for several moments. "How come you know where the two ships are, but they don't know where you are?"

Concern spread across the admiral's face. "They don't know where we are *yet*." He breathed deeply. "We watched the jump gate, so when they came through, we saw them. Also, they're doing sensor sweeps that we can easily plot." He rubbed his chin.

"And, I suspect they're looking for you, not us." Leonidas stepped closer to the display and Justin followed. Pointing to the planet he said, "Your small vessel was last seen near Lepanto, so that is where they started looking." He gestured to a group of three blue dots nearby. "We pulled back the few ships we had in that area. The bulk of our fleet is on the edge of the system and in emcon, not radiating anything except excess heat. However, those two ships," he pointed toward the two red dots, "will eventually find us."

"But Exodus can stop them, right?"

"No. All this ship has are a few missile launchers and anti-missile defense guns we installed after capturing it."

"Oh." In an instant Justin's mind raced through possible options, none of them good.

"But, if we are forced into a fight, the other ships in the battle group will destroy them."

"Forced into a fight?"

Both men turned at the sound of Naomi's voice.

"You are not going to be forced to fight. The recon ship will jump away at the first hint of trouble. That class of ships always has their FTL engines spun up, ready to jump."

Leonidas bit his lip and stared at her. "I doubt the pirates will fight the Titan fleet."

Justin shook his head. *Ferren fight a fleet?* "Not a chance."

The admiral nodded. "If they won't attack us, all we need is time to get away from here." He turned to one of the nearby technicians. "Contact Admiral Cottrell." As soon as he appeared, Leonidas conveyed the new information.

The merest hint of a smile broached the other admiral's face. "If we destroy the jump gate, it will slow down the arrival of reinforcements."

Leonidas agreed.

"I'll have it done the moment we're discovered."

Nearly an hour later, the two intruders were on an arcing course toward the fleet when a technician announced, "Target ships are approaching scanning range."

Leonidas gave a slight nod and ordered all heat exchangers turned off.

"We have been scanned. Initiating scan counter measures."

Justin expected alarms, shouts, frantic action and commands, but nothing like that happened.

"Lock on, but hold your fire," Leonidas said calmly. "Maintain emcon and jam any transmissions."

Mr. Green smiled broadly. "They certainly weren't expecting us. There's near panic on the pirate ship."

Leonidas grinned then shot a glance from Naomi back to Green. "What's the situation on the recon ship?"

A red flash from the holo display caught Justin's eye.

"The jump gate has been destroyed," a technician advised.

Before Mr. Green could answer, another man said, "Both ships have jumped sir."

Moments later the two ships appeared where the gate had been seconds before. The recon ship immediately jumped again. Just as the Titan fleet had done, it was now hiding somewhere nearby. Ferren's ship was less swift. Under the guns of a Titan battleship, the Acheron took minutes to spin up their FTL drive and flee. Justin delighted in imagining the sweat pouring down the fat pirate's face as his crew madly worked to jump away.

Leonidas smiled. Relief spread across his face. "Secure from general quarters and set condition two, throughout the ship. Remember people," he said raising his voice and looking up and down the compartment, "those ships are either hiding nearby or fleeing as best they can. They will probably return—with help. Stay alert." Then he turned to Naomi and said, "Thank you for your assistance."

Crewmembers opened some hatches. Justin and Naomi wheeled Mara back to the clinic with the medic and Thor not far behind.

Because of the closed hatches, they followed a different path out of the superstructure. As they wound their way back, they crossed paths with a squad of Marines and dogs. Thor locked eyes with the officer just as he seemed about to question them.

The marine looked at them with a mixture of surprise and amazement. "You're the ones they found on Lepanto?"

Justin nodded, amazed that the dog had evidently conveyed that message.

"I thought it was just rumors, stories." After a brief discussion, the marines escorted them, opening hatches along the way.

Arriving at the clinic the medic checked in. Becca greeted them on the ward then did a quick check of her patient. "After my shift I'll bring Mara to my quarters." Her bright eyes glancing between Naomi and Justin she said, "I'll see you both there for dinner, okay?"

They all agreed, but no one moved. Becca looked from person to person with a confused expression.

"So, are we really sisters?" Mara finally asked with a gesture toward Naomi.

"Yes," Becca said with a surprised look. "You didn't know?"

Mara shook her head. "Did everyone know—except us?"

"Everyone who read the med or intel reports." Becca called up their medical records on a nearby screen. "When you were brought in the Lepanto medical team did routine workups on all of you. That included DNA swabs. The information was uploaded to the med computer for more detailed analysis." For several moments, she examined the two records. "See," she said pointing to the DNA profiles, "you share the same parents—you're sisters."

The two looked at each other, but neither smiled.

"That's good isn't it?" Becca asked.

"Yes." Naomi said without emotion.

Mara shrugged. "How could we be sisters?"

Justin thought for several moments then, looking at Naomi, said, "The story you were told about the Titan ship that was attacked, the crew venting the atmosphere, and being cloned from DNA found on the ship…."

Naomi shook her head. "That must be a lie."

"Not all of it. Being on a ship under attack and left in an escape pod…."

"My earliest memory," Mara said as surprise spread across her face. "Were we all on that ship?"

"Yes," Justin said. "They must have tried to save the children."

"Do you know how old you are?" Mara asked.

"They told me twenty-two."

"I'm twenty-four—little sister."

The two women stared at each other for several moments as tears welled in their eyes. Then Naomi bent down and they hugged each other.

"I need to get Mara to treatment." Becca breathed deeply and wiped her eye. "I'll see you both at dinner tonight."

Justin nodded, took Naomi by the hand, and left the room.

They walked in silence to the docking station where she had first arrived, but instead of taking a shuttle headed for another ship, he took her down one level to a subway system that ran the length and circumference of Exodus. Fifteen minutes after boarding, they disembarked at a small station surrounded by orchard trees. A dirt path took them away from the station, through the grove.

"Becca took me here a couple of days ago." As they walked along the path, shaded by fruit trees, he said, "She told me she comes here to figure things out."

"Figure things out," she mumbled.

Several minutes later, they came out of the trees. Now, on one side of the path, corn grew head high, on the other side wheat stood nearly as tall.

Up ahead men worked on machinery in the mud of a fallow field. Naomi stopped and stared. "Titan soldiers obeying the commands of a pregnant norm and working as farmers in the mud." Her expression turned angry. "Is all of our history a lie?"

## Chapter 20

Justin shrugged. "I don't know that I can answer that, *yet*, but I'm convinced the truth is more complex than the stories we've been taught. This fleet easily could have destroyed the Acheron and the imperial recon vessel, but they didn't. Why would rogue killers show restraint?"

Naomi appeared deep in thought as she shook her head.

"The only conclusion that makes sense is that the Titans aren't crazed killers."

She nodded. "They are more normal than I expected…more normal than the Nephilim and far less creepy." Her expression changed from thoughtful to serious. "We need answers. Do you believe Becca will tell us the truth?"

"As she knows it, yes."

"Then tonight should be most revealing."

He smiled. "Until then let's try and enjoy the day."

They continued past orchards and fields. Hand-in-hand they turned onto one intersecting path and then another. Only occasionally did they meet a worker operating some sort of farm equipment. Justin felt refreshed to be outside and in the country, even if it wasn't actually outside. As they walked they discussed the unlikely events that had brought them to this place and talked of nothing as they strolled casually to nowhere.

After turning down another path, Naomi said, "Let's head back to the rail station and go somewhere else."

Justin didn't recognize any of the fields or building that were now in view, but he didn't want to admit it to her. "I think the station is this way."

Naomi gave him a skeptical look.

After walking half a kilometer, they came to a road. Justin stopped on the edge and tried to get his bearings. A line of twenty people, adults, teens and a few younger children, approached in single file. Each wore a white robe.

*Where have I seen robes like that?* Finally, he recalled that monks in ancient times had worn similar outfits.

"Why are they dressed so funny?" Naomi whispered.

Justin explained what he knew and together they watched the strange parade. Suddenly he squeezed Naomi's hand. "That's him—Mr. Blue, from the interrogation I told you about that first day here. Let's follow him."

"Sure," Naomi smiled. "He probably knows where he is going."

Justin ignored her and fell in behind as the last monk passed by.

After about an hour of moving slowly and silently, they reached the edge of a community. Mothers pulled children out of the way, others stepped aside, trolleys and equipment stopped so the monks could proceed straight down the street.

Near the center of the community, they came to a one-story circular building with no windows. As they approached, a young boy and girl held two large doors open and the line of monks moved silently in.

Justin pointed above the doors. "The same fish like symbol that is on your medallion."

Naomi clutched her breast and nodded.

The two children followed into the building and the doors closed behind them.

Justin stepped forward.

"You are not going in. Are you?"

"Sure, why not?"

Words stumbled from her. "It is not a public building."

"It doesn't say private." He marched forward.

"They will probably kill us both."

"You don't believe that," Justin said over his shoulder.

Gently pulling heavy doors, Justin peeked within. The hallway followed the curve of the building disappearing in both directions. As they stepped inside, a long stand stood immediately in front, holding an open book. He examined it.

"The Prophecies of Justin." He pulled a copy from his pocket. "It's some sort of holy book to the Titans."

Naomi sneered.

Looking for where the monks might have gone, Justin stepped to the right. Instantly, six young men blocked his way.

He stepped back. Where did they come from?

Naomi drew close to him, fists at the ready.

The men, each in gis with black belts, stood in a semi-circle about them. Justin wondered if they had somehow blinded him for a moment. They stood like statues, providing only one option, to retreat through the doors they had entered.

"Welcome to our school." Mr. Green walked up clad in a white robe. Pulling the hood from his head, he looked at them, then hinted a smile. "We don't normally do tours."

Naomi, tense like a lioness ready to pounce, said, "Sorry. We will leave."

"That will not be necessary, if you have come to learn." He casually flipped the pages of the book. "Have you read it?"

"No," Justin replied. "I'd like to, but I've been busy."

Green shook his head in obvious disappointment. Flipping to the back he said, "The last page is particularly instructive." He walked away. As he was about to disappear around the bend of the hall he said, "If you are interested in truth, come with me."

The gi-clad silent sentinels stepped aside allowing Justin to follow and, with a shake of her head, Naomi trailed behind. Together they passed classrooms and labs filled with students. Moments later, they came to a young woman holding open an elevator door.

Once inside Green said, "I don't believe we have been properly introduced. I am General Olham."

"No," Justin replied. "I've always just thought of you as Mr. Green."

Olham laughed. "And did you call your other interrogator, Mr. Blue?"

Justin nodded. "And I suspect you know our names."

"Yes, I do," he said with a big smile. "Observation balcony."

"What do you do here?" Justin asked as the elevator dropped beneath his feet. *Worse than an FTL jump.*

"As I said, this is a school. We teach psychic skills here. I am Dean of the Adepts."

"Adepts?"

"You call them shadow warriors…"

Justin struggled to hide the fear that spiked within him.

"…but that is only part of what we teach. Like any human ability, Titan psychic powers exist in a range. Most people are average, some are above and a few are truly adept. Student that earn the white robe are called Adepts. Think of what I do as advanced level training for the gifted. Some of those talented people become shadow warriors."

The elevator slowed and then stopped. Stepping from it, they entered a tiny room. Olham opened one of two doors and walked onto a balcony.

With Naomi close behind, Justin followed. He looked down a deep shaft. At the bottom was a circle of white-robed monks.

"What is this place and what are they doing?"

"Originally this facility was part of a science academy. The designers planned the shaft and the observation bubble at the bottom, as a means to access experiments outside the protective hull of the ship."

Looking down the shaft Naomi asked, "Outside the hull? Unshielded?"

"The room is still protected from solar radiation, but for a telepath it is the quietest place on the ship. Your other interrogator that day, Major Rasnic, is one of our finest instructors. He's down there now with some of our best students searching for the two intruder ships."

"They're still out there?"

Olham turned to Justin and with sadness in his voice said, "They're out there, afraid and desperately trying to contact help."

"Do you feel sorry for them?" Naomi asked.

"No." He shook his head. "Being an empath is one of the talents of a true Adept. The two ships are hiding out there, at the edge of the solar system, but I can still feel their fear."

Naomi's eyes widened. "At that distance?"

"Yes. As they approached I established a link with them and have kept it active since, reading their thoughts when they were closer, now just their emotions."

Justin looked down at the Adepts and shook his head. "I wouldn't want such ability. It would be a burden."

"Talent often comes with burdens, but Adepts often achieve one great benefit."

"Oh?" Justin looked at the older man.

"Once in a while when we meditate or pray, we sense the presence of God and for those moments we are willing to endure the fear, pain, and suffering, we often feel from those around us." Olham looked at both of them and grinned. "I don't need to be an Adept to see your disbelief. If you are willing to train with us you might glimpse what I mean."

"No thank you." Naomi quickly interjected. "I have already experienced too much religious silliness while in the empire." She backed away. "I am leaving."

"I'll be with you in a moment." Justin watched her leave and then turned to Olham. "I should go with her, but I want to know the truth. When could I come back and start training?"

"Tomorrow at dawn."

"Dawn?" He took a deep breath. "Okay."

Minutes later, back at the entrance, he walked up to the book. Still open to the end page he read the last line.

*Titan history begins when we meet at Lepanto. Come quickly. Amen.*

He shook his head and walked away.

\*　　\*　　\*

Justin caught up with Naomi at the rail station. They rode back together, but mainly in silence. He decided not to tell her about his plan to return to the school.

Arriving at Becca's quarters, they were greeted by Mara, standing at the door. "Hi. Becca and Jon are in the kitchen." She walked a few steps and sat down.

Justin turned to Mara about to say how well she looked when Becca appeared in a doorway.

"Welcome, both of you. We'll be out in a moment." Seconds later, Becca and Jon brought several bowls of food, a large loaf of bread and pitcher of water to the dining room. After introductions, they all sat around the table dishing up food and talking. Jon, like every Titan Justin had seen, was tall, trim and well proportioned. His close-cropped brown hair had a slight wave to it. Jon, a full head higher than Becca, moved to the table with others. Taking the seat beside his wife, he passed one food bowl to her and another to Mara.

Waiting for one of the bowls to get to him Justin turned to Jon. "I know that Becca is a doctor and a good one judging from the progress Mara has made, but what do you do?"

"I'm an FTL engineer."

He nodded. "That's a good job."

"Frustrating is what it is. We think we have the new engines properly assembled and installed, but they require a human pilot for initialization. We've never found the interface or the plans." He flushed just a bit. "We even searched your ship, but…well we never found one so we don't know how it works."

Justin looked at Mara, but said nothing.

Jon followed his gaze and asked Mara, "Are you an FTL engineer?"

She shook her head.

"The human interface, are you familiar with it?"

Mara nodded. "Very."

"Do you know what one looks like? Can you give us a diagram?"

"I can't diagram it but," she pulled up her hair, "it looks like this."

## Chapter 21

Jon's jaw dropped, as did the spoon in his hand. "Ahhhh…"

Apparently enjoying the reaction, Mara chuckled, let her hair fall and turned to Becca. "The food looks lovely." She reached for the salad bowl.

"Can I, ah, how does it…." Jon took a deep breath. "Perhaps we could…." He turned to his wife, "Why didn't you tell me about this?"

"You're the engineer. You think I knew what that thing was? I'm a doctor. It had nothing to do with her injury. I noted it and moved on. And besides, Mara is my patient. I can't go telling you things about her."

Jon continued his stumbling request for Mara's assistance.

Justin wanted to ask his sister to help them, but would she be willing? She seemed calm, even amused, sitting across the table from a very animated Titan, but just days ago, she had tried to kill herself when she realized she was one.

Becca sighed and placed her hand on her husband's, stopping his ramble. "Mara, I'm sure you've read my thoughts over the last few days. I hope you've learned that the Titans aren't the monsters that you've been taught."

"I have been reading your thoughts. I don't know how to stop."

Justin made a mental note to teach her.

"It's because of your thoughts that I will help. Seeing your love for Jon and seeing history through your eyes, I understand that what I thought I knew must be wrong."

"Or simply a lie," Naomi added.

Jon looked at Becca and Mara. "Thank you, both." He touched his wife's shoulder, "Can I borrow your patient tomorrow?"

"Yes, but I'm coming with her."

Jon gave his wife an approving nod then picked up the loaf of bread and broke it in two. "May the God of Justin and this house, bless this meal and our guests." He leaned back in his chair and dished up food.

Ensuring his mind was closed to those around him, Justin pondered the meaning of the simple blessing. Long before the Alien and Titanomachy wars, belief in science and reason had supplanted the supernatural. *Whatever else the Titans were when they left Earth on their long journey to war, they had certainly been atheists, but today, faith is woven into their culture. Were they killers early on, but time and a belief in the supernatural had changed them? Perhaps tomorrow I'll learn the...*

"Come on Justin." Naomi thumped his arm. "Must I tell the whole story?"

"Huh?" Justin reached for his fork.

"Naomi was telling us how you got lost today," Mara said.

"I wasn't lost." Justin gave his version of events and reached for the interesting cheese dish that seemed to be the main course.

After several minutes of eating and small talk, Naomi turned to Becca. "How many norm humans are in the Titan fleet?"

"I'm one of the last. The Titan genes have never been isolated, but they're dominant. If one parent is Titan, the child has psychic abilities."

"So both your parents were norms?"

"Yes. They were doctors working in the colonies. EarthGov drafted them to treat Titan wounded toward the end of the Alien War."

"They were only with the Titans because they were drafted?"

"At first, but by the end of the war, my parents understood that Titans were, well, human. After that war, Titans were ordered to return for decommissioning, but it didn't take long to learn that decommissioning meant killing." She took her husband's hand. "My parents sided with the Titans and I'm glad they did."

"Why would EarthGov want to kill their own soldiers?" Naomi looked doubtful.

Becca shrugged.

"How can we know the motives of others?" Jon took a deep breath. "Many people think they had grown afraid of us."

"They do fear you…us," Justin said. It all made sense. Nearly a million experienced combat veterans, now with psychic powers, returning to Earth. If they were allowed to integrate back into society, they could easily take over the Confederation—if they wanted to. So, EarthGov planned to kill them as they came back for decommissioning. But, the Titans discovered the plan and fought back—the Titanomachy War. Justin wanted to ponder it deeper but, as he looked around the table, everyone ate in silence. *I need to lighten things up.* Looking at Becca he asked, "Could we meet your parents?"

She frowned. "My mother went on the vanguard mission to Lepanto. My father died just last year."

Justin bit his lip. *Well that didn't work.* "I'm sorry to hear that."

Silence hung heavy for several moments only broken when Naomi asked, "Could I get a slate? I want to read the history of the Titans from the Titan point of view."

"I'll get you one after dinner," Becca said. "The Alien and Titanomachy wars will be very different than the history you have been taught."

"You should read the history of the Prophet," Jon added. "That is a vital part of who we are as Titans."

"I will," Naomi said.

The conversation lagged and Mara asked, "What else can we talk about?"

*Something that's not a political or emotional minefield.* Justin decided to let someone else try for a topic.

Mara took a bite of her food and chewed slowly. "Since we are Titans we must be related to people in the fleet."

A smile spread across Becca's face. "Yes, you must." She asked her husband to clear the dishes while she retrieved her slate from a nearby table. With fingers flitting across the screen she asked, "Do all three of you want to know what I find?"

Everyone nodded.

Mere moments later, she stopped. "Well this is interesting."

"What?" Justin asked. He looked at Naomi. "Are we all cousins?"

"No." She paused still staring at the screen. "It's just…the intel division has already done the DNA genealogy on all of you."

Why would they do that? "What did they find?"

"Well, Mara and Naomi, you're related to a family on the transport ship Victorious. I don't know them, but I'll send the contact information to the slate we give you."

Naomi grinned. "I can imagine our first meeting. Hello, we are your relatives from four hundred years in the future."

Becca's fingers came to a sudden halt. "This just gets more interesting all the time!"

Mara gasped, then looked at Becca and blushed. "Sorry. I can't stop reading your thoughts."

"I'm used to it—believe me. Justin, you're a direct descendant of Leonidas."

"Leonidas?" He let the information soak in for several moments. Leonidas? His living ancestor was the most reviled mass murderer in the empire and CFS.

Jon reached across the table and touched his hand. "Leonidas was…is a great man. He saved us all when he led the mission to capture Exodus. Becca told me what you've been taught. It's not true."

*True? What is truth?* At the moment, he wasn't sure he knew the answer. He felt numb.

"Do you want to leave?" Naomi asked.

He shook his head. "It's just going to take time to sort out."

Looking at Justin, Mara said, "Perhaps we should talk about something else."

Jon nodded. "We have a cocoon," He looked at Mara, "The place you lie when connected to the ship. That's what you call it, right?"

Mara, her mouth full, nodded.

"We found it on a wreck in the debris field. We were still trying to figure it out when your ship landed. We used the one on your ship as a guide to repair it."

Becca patted his hand. "Save that one for later." Without waiting for a reply, she turned to the others. "There was an announcement this morning that the ship will be at its closest to the Lepanto sun tomorrow." Her face seemed to light up. "There's going to be a praise and thanksgiving celebration and Leonidas said he will open the sky shutters. We'll be able to see the sun."

"Why is being close to the sun a cause for celebration?" Mara asked.

"Well, one reason is that many of us have never seen a star."

Justin was still trying to figure out exactly what she meant when Jon explained.

"Actually, everyone has seen them as tiny points of light, but most people my age or younger have no memory of a sun as other than a distant star." Gesturing toward his wife he added, "We were infants during the Titanomachy War. Because of my work retrieving engine parts, I have been in the habitable zone of the Lepanto sun, felt its warmth and seen it as a fiery orb."

"But," Becca leaned forward, "the most important reason is that Justin tells us that it was here in the Lepanto system, with his Titan brothers and sisters, that he came to know God."

Justin raised an eyebrow. "Have Titans been here before?"

"No." Becca shook her head. "Well, other than our vanguard mission."

"But this prophet you talk about, didn't he die hundreds of years ago?"

"Yes," Jon nodded.

"Then how could he say it was here that he met God?"

Jon shook his head. "We don't know. It's a mystery, but many are convinced that the Prophet will return when the fleet reaches periapsis, the closest point to the sun."

Justin tightly closed his mind to those around him before allowing himself to mull that idea. A man dead for six hundred years, miraculously reappears here, hundreds of light years from where he lived, and somehow encounters God. Justin glanced at Naomi. Her face betrayed not a hint of emotion, but he could imagine the skepticism and sarcasm that boiled in her well-shielded mind. Mara merely looked confused. Justin grinned. "I guess we'll know tomorrow."

## Chapter 22

I'm not just a Titan, I'm the descendant of their genocidal leader. Justin shook his head. *But, Leonidas doesn't seem like a killer. He seems harmless.* Using a borrowed slate, Justin navigated his way through the superstructure's labyrinth of passageways, to the cabin of Leonidas. *He admitted to being the leader of the attack on Earth, but he doesn't seem to be in charge now. Why is Admiral Cottrell giving orders? More questions to ask.* Justin yawned and fatigue swept over him like a wave, but he pressed on.

As if he had a fairy resting in his hand, the image of a woman appeared atop the slate. "Turn right and proceed 10 meters down the passageway."

Staring at the image, he turned and stumbled over a dog. Managing to stay afoot he said, "Sorry." *There I go talking to dogs again. It almost seems normal now.* He stopped, turned, and watched the animal trot down the hall. *Why are dogs telepathic? How did that happen?* With a shake of the head, he continued on his way. He looked down as the little woman in his hand pointed and told him to go left. He turned and looked up in time to come nose-to-nose with a guard.

"You have arrived," the little woman said and disappeared.

*Thanks.* He stepped back.

"Can I help you, sir?" The guard, about his age, stood against the wall in an entryway.

"I'm...ah...Justin Garrett."

The guard announced him over an intercom and he was quickly admitted.

"Welcome. Sit down," Leonidas urged.

Standing just inside the door, he found himself in the living room. Chairs formed a semi-circle around a low table covered with papers. Leonidas gestured toward one of the seats. A tiny kitchen area stood against the back wall and in a corner a neatly kept desk. To the left a door led, he assumed, to a bedroom and bathroom. The quarters were larger than Becca and Jon's, but smaller than his old quarters on Liberty. *More than comfortable for one man.*

"The guard wasn't surprised to see me." *Well, after I got out of his face.* "Did you know I was coming?"

He shook his head. "I knew eventually you would come and the sentries were told to admit you whenever you appeared. Sit down. Would you like anything?"

*A good stiff drink.* "No." He sat.

"I was going to contact you. Your ship will be ready late tomorrow." Leonidas sat across from him. "Do you still want to leave?"

"How long have you known we were related."

"The intel people on Lepanto discovered you were a Titan and shortly thereafter they determined that we were related." The old man looked intently at Justin with a sad smile. "That is why you were brought to this ship."

"You knew when we met that first day?"

He nodded.

"Why didn't you tell me?"

"I almost did, but you weren't handling what I had already told you all that well."

Justin remembered running from the plaza when Leo told him he was Admiral Leonidas.

"I decided to let you find out the truth in your own time."

Thor trotted in and curled up on the floor between them.

Justin asked about dog's telepathic abilities.

"They seem to have always had those skills."

Justin's eyebrow rose.

"We've done some genetic work on them, raising their intelligence a bit, lengthening average lifespan several years, but the psychic abilities were there from the start. I've wondered if other animals back on Earth have similar abilities."

Justin pondered it all while staring at Thor.

The dog stared back with his tongue hanging out to the side.

The old man reached over and petted the dog. "Thor was Simon's dog." He paused for a moment then said, "Simon was my youngest son. I think I told you that he went on the vanguard mission."

Justin nodded and for nearly a minute, they sat together in silence. "How did the Titanomachy War begin?"

Leonidas sighed then told much the same version as Jon and Becca had a few hours earlier. Anger flared in his voice as he ended. "When we were ordered back many said we would be betrayed. It was what the Prophet told us. I didn't believe them. We had defeated the Grays in the Alien War. We deserved honor and praise, but instead we were murdered."

"Why did Titans attack Earth? You had a fleet of ships. Why not just leave."

"That's what we wanted to do, but we had almost a million soldiers in captured alien territory or in the colonies. We were bringing them back to staging areas, but the only ship capable of moving them all at once, out of norm-controlled space, was in orbit around Earth."

"Terra Nova."

Leonidas nodded. "Exodus. We hoped to capture it and leave the norms behind. No more fear. No more war. No more killing." His eyes welled with tears.

The old man had once told Justin that years earlier he had a wife and four sons. One son went on the vanguard mission, but the others? "Your wife and three sons, they died in the Battle of Earth?"

The admiral nodded.

Justin reached out and touched his hand. "One son lived, loved and had children, Simon my ancestor." There were more questions, but he had all the answers he needed for now. He stood, rested a hand on the admiral's shoulder, and said, "Thank you for fixing the ship, but we won't be leaving."

\* \* \*

The skylights glowed dimly as Justin arrived for his first day of formal, psychic training. Fitful sleep had provided little rest. He strained to open one of the school's great doors. Once inside he approached the Prophet's book, still open to the last page, and began to read.

*I race to Lepanto where my Titan brothers and sisters will be.*

*I did not know You then, but You knew me.*

*I will stand among the brothers and sisters, but I will not see You.*

*When the light drives out the darkness You will be there with me, but no one will see You.*

*Reluctantly I will walk the path You lay before me, but You will be patient.*

*I came toward Lepanto not knowing You, but I will serve You before I leave.*

*I am content.*

*Titan history begins when we meet at Lepanto. Come quickly. Amen.*

Pulling his copy of the prophecies from his side pocket, he wondered if all of it was as confusing as these few lines.

"Have you read it?"

Startled, Justin turned to see the white robed man beside him. "Good morning, Olham. Yes, a little more since we last talked. I can't say that I understand it. Why did he write it so...cryptically?"

"You've been reading the harder parts." Stepping up to the volume, he turned to the first page. "Start at the beginning. The Prophet describes his first meeting with God. We don't know where this happened, but Justin and his friend Jon are imprisoned by his enemies. Jon guides Justin to faith before he is killed." Olham flipped through the pages slowly. "He struggles to understand the mission God has sent before him. He argues that he is unworthy and unable but, in the end, he journeys to those Titans of long ago and tells them of a loving, caring God that we can know."

"But the last part?"

He turned to the end. "These are the actual prophecies. The Prophet saw that we would receive psychic abilities and that they would be both a burden and gift. The Prophet said to be wary of norm leaders because they would betray us, but many of the less powerful would help us."

"And those things came true," he mumbled thoughtfully. Then he shook his head. "But I don't understand...the last page?"

"It says he will be here with us, but exactly what it means, well, I don't think we were meant to know—until after the event." He shrugged. "Perhaps we will understand it later today." He gave Justin a fatherly smile, gestured down the hall, and said, "Are you ready for your first lesson?"

He remained skeptical about the Titan religion. He doubted the Prophet would miraculously appear later that day, but if he did, Justin wanted to be there. "Will you be at the celebration?" he asked Olham.

"Wouldn't miss it."

Justin nodded and followed him down the hall.

They entered a small gymnasium about ten meters square. Olham opened a locker in the wall, pulled out a staff and pair of goggles and handed them to Justin.

The goggles had dark lens. Justin put them on his head, but not over his eyes.

"When we begin, the lights will dim and white noise will fill the room. You won't be able to see or hear anything. Your goal is to find me. I'll stand at some spot and you point the staff at where you believe I am. If you are successful, I'll move around. Are you ready?"

Justin nodded and pulled the goggles down over his eyes. He knew, from years of experience, that he could sense people on the other side of a door or around a corner. Olham soon recognized his ability and moved around the room at an ever-quicker pace. Later still, Olham donned goggles and both men used their minds to find and tag the other. Hours later Justin's head hurt and he struggled to focus on the increasingly harder tasks. He was glad when Olham said it was time to stop.

Together Justin and his teacher traveled to the stadium. He wanted Naomi to go with him to the celebration, but she declined saying she would be studying the history and religion of the Titans. She assured him that the Prophet would not be there. He suspected that she was right, but still wanted to see the event.

Due to the threat from imperial ships, Jon and his team worked on the FTL engines every day. Mara was probably on the bridge with him. As Justin walked the last few meters to the arena he imagined Mara in the cocoon with Jon nervously hovering around her. *Mara hates the interface, but loves the attention.*

Even from the outside, it was clear the site of the celebration was huge. The curve of the stadium was hardly visible as they came up from the rail station. He could see thousands pouring in through dozens of entrances.

Once inside Olham led him high in the stands.

"This is the stadium where we hold major sporting events and celebrations."

They entered an elevator with others and within moments, it shot upward.

Justin took a deep breath and let it out slowly.

Olham pointed the way forward. "The senior staff shares a box at the upper level. Leonidas asked me to bring you up if you attended."

Queasy, he nodded, not even attempting to speak.

Once inside the skybox Justin spotted Leonidas sitting up front. Officers flanked him on either side. Olham walked forward and spoke to the admiral. Within moments, two seats were made available beside Leonidas.

Justin felt like a man at the edge of a cliff looking down at people in a deep valley. Tens of thousands packed the seats and thousands filled the field.

Sitting beside Justin, Olham gestured toward the crowd. "People have come from all the other ships to be here for this moment."

Giant screens displayed a choral group at the far end as they prepared to sing. "When does it begin?"

"When the sky shutters start to open," Leonidas said pointing up.

The thousands on the field swayed back and forth as if they were a single entity as an A cappella song rose spontaneously from the crowd. Quickly it spread throughout the arena even to many in the skybox.

*Holy, Holy, Holy!*

*You remembered us even when we did not know You.*

*You are the creator, we are Your creation*

*You are forever, we are the momentary*

*Holy, Holy, Holy!*

*You remembered us even when we did not know You.*

*You are the God of the Prophet.*

*Remember us as we remember You*

*Holy, Holy, Holy!*

The huge sky shutters, locked in place for more than twenty years, creaked and moaned as they inched open.

All went dark.

## Chapter 23

Startled, Justin shot to his feet. Shrieks and shouts rose from the crowd as his eyes searched the darkness. Quickly he became aware of lights sprinkled about, some over exits and others in the crowd. A spotlight came on, and then another, bathing the stage in a harsh white light. Looking over the top of the stadium, he could see lights in the nearby buildings. Casting his gaze still farther, he could see distant stars through the still-opening shutters. *They turned the sky lights out as they opened skylight portals.* Smiling he turned to Olham.

The teacher gave Justin a quizzical look. "I will stand among the brothers and sisters, but I will not see You."

"What? Why are you quoting that?"

He shook his head and looked up at the growing view of stars.

Justin, firmly gripped the railing as he watched the crowd below. The stars glided across the open sky and within seconds an eerie glow grew in intensity. As the first golden beams of light reached down, the crowd sent up a deafening roar. The group on stage sang, "Holy, Holy, Holy," as a second dawn graced the day.

"When the light drives out the darkness You will be there with me, but no one will see You," Olham again quoted the prophet.

A prayerful roar spread through the crowd at the end of the first hymn. Many glanced up at the sun, but most seemed to bath in the warm glow.

Through several hymns Justin stood, eyes closed, and let the emotions of the crowd flow through him in a way he had never before experienced. Finally, as the rotation of the ship brought a new dawn he sat.

A man walked to center stage and lifted his arms into the sunlight.

"Who is that?" Justin asked.

Olham shrugged. "There are many people from other ships here today."

As the singing faded the man on stage dropped his arms and looked out at the crowd. "God, has told us, through his Prophet, that when the light drives out the darkness he will be there with us, but we will not see him. We are also told that through some miracle the Prophet is here and that our history begins now." He shook his head. "I don't claim to understand any of that, but I know God's word is true. He told us we would be betrayed and that we would make it here to this place." He lifted his arms into the air, "And I know that when this light fades his light will still shine on us."

The singing continued, but as Exodus pulled away from the Lepanto sun, the light waned as well as the excitement of the crowd.

Leonidas turned to Justin, "It's been good to see you again, but I've got to get back to the bridge. With the help of Mara, we hope to test the FTL engines tomorrow." Others departed with him. Soon only Olham sat with Justin in the skybox.

Justin stayed behind with a growing sense of disappointment. So many had hoped for the return of the prophet, but as the sun slipped ever more toward the stern of the ship. No one miraculously appeared before the crowd. As the shutters closed, the crowd slowly dispersed.

Olham leaned toward Justin, "Will I see you tomorrow for your next lesson?"

Justin nodded and followed him from the box. Together they reached the main floor and joined the throng leaving the stadium. Around them people expressed their doubts and questions. "Where is Justin?" "Where is the Prophet?" "If they do not appear is it all a lie?" Their doubts seemed to infect him. *Where was the Prophet? Was there a prophet? Is there a god?* He would have liked a miracle to dispel his doubts. He turned to ask Olham a question, but his teacher had disappeared in the multitude. Alone Justin walked through the crowd.

Sluggishly, he wandered toward the rail station and then to his empty room. He didn't know why, but he felt the need to be with friends. There was no answer at Mara and Naomi's quarters. He had no idea where Naomi might be, but Mara should be in the cocoon on the bridge. He had never been there, but he was sure he could find it.

Usually civilians were not admitted, but when he arrived at the bridge, the guard allowed him to pass. Once inside he found Mara plugged into the cocoon and Becca hovering over her like a worried mother.

After greeting him Becca said, "Her vital signs are good, but is it normal for pilots to sleep in the cocoon?"

Justin looked down at Mara lying in the pod and nodded. From long experience, he knew that she was analyzing lines of code and testing controls. "She isn't really sleeping, just busy."

Moments later Becca's eyes widened as the image of Mara appeared and began discussing system specifications with Jon.

Justin grinned at her astonishment. It was then that he noticed Naomi sitting at a table off to the side of the bridge.

As he approached, she looked up. "Did you see the Prophet? God maybe?"

"Sarcasm does not become you. What are you doing?"

"I may not believe in any gods or prophets, but what I found while studying today convinced me that the Titans…our people…are telling the truth." With sad eyes she looked silently off in the distance. After several moments she continued, "I decided to help by drawing the various imperial ships for the intel people."

He looked at her crude drawings and pointed to his head, "Send me a mental image of the ship." She did and taking the slate she used, he began to sketch. "What did you find that convinced you?"

She sighed and again sadness filled her face. "Drawings and a photo."

Justin looked confused.

"I found them in the central archive. I copied them onto the slate back at my quarters, but I need more time to understand them." She pointed to Justin's sketch, "Gun ports there and there."

"But these drawings convinced you?"

She nodded. "Particle cannon on the bow here."

"I'd like to see the drawings you found."

"Give me a couple of days to finish researching them."

He agreed and handed the slate to her. She typed in the class, top speed, duration, and other details she could recall and then saved the file.

After more than an hour of work she said, "This final class of ship was my home for the last several years."

Forming in his mind was the image of long slender vessel wrapping around a central sphere. Numerous nacelles indicated the stern of the craft.

"This is a Temple class vessel. The Nephilim use these as command ships."

"I get the sense that it is huge."

She nodded. "Not as vast as Exodus, but still enormous. 9,000 meters in length, much better armed and fast."

"A ship that large and still fast?"

"The engines create a gravitational vortex that distorts space-time. Over short distances, a few million kilometers, travel is instantaneous."

As he drew, Justin struggled to imagine such a ship. Surfeit, the ship they had stolen from Galt, was a mere 250 meters in length. Most CFS warships were less than a 1,000 meters. Titan warships appeared to be of similar size. The ship he was on might be twice as long as a Temple ship, but Exodus had minimal weapons and, until they got the engines fixed, it was slower than many sub-light pleasure craft.

"There are gun ports every ten meters along the keel and a large particle cannon at the bow." She waited for him to finish drawing then added, "The ship has four sensor dishes built into the hull of the vessel, on the bow, stern, port. and starboard." She pointed to each spot. "The dishes are very distinctive. They have the insignia of the Imperial Navy above them and the emblem of the Nephilim painted on the dome."

"Dish? Dome? I'm confused about what you mean."

She concentrated and the image of a huge sensor dish covered by a protective dome formed in his mind. "Four bulging eyes covered with an eyelid. Got it." He began to draw. "I've heard of triple redundancy, but quadruple?"

"It is not quite redundant, if one is destroyed it creates a blind spot."

"So it has a weakness."

"Every vessel has a weakness. That is why they build different types, but I would not want to fight this ship. The Nephilim spare no expense for their protection."

The two quickly finished up and handed the pad to Leonidas.

He looked at each carefully and asked questions. "Nice drawings. Thank you. I'll get the intel division to download the information into our database." He handed it to an aide. "The repair crew has brought your ship alongside Exodus. They told me that some secondary systems still need repair and the FTL drive hasn't been fueled. You said the other day you won't be leaving, do you still want the craft?"

Naomi touched his hand. *You never know when you might need a ship.*

A grin slowly spread across Justin's face. "I stole it, I might as well keep it."

Leonidas smiled.

Naomi let Justin feel her satisfaction, then excused herself and left the bridge.

"I can work on the electronics," Justin said, "but I'm sure you don't let just anyone handle anti-matter, so, how do I get the ship fueled?"

The admiral called Jon over and explained the situation to him.

"I should be able to do it tomorrow. We're making fantastic progress." He turned to Justin, "Mara has been a great help. I'll meet you at the shuttle port first thing in the morning."

Justin thanked them both and walked over to where a holographic image of Mara talked with several technicians. "How are you doing?"

"Great. I see that Surfeit has been brought alongside Exodus."

"How did you know that? I thought you were just working on the FTL systems?"

"I got bored waiting for the engines to initialize and spin up and wanted to see and hear what was around me so I entered the sensor and comm systems."

"What do they think about that?" he said, gesturing toward the two technicians nearby.

"As long as I fix their engines I don't think they care what I do."

Justin laughed. "I'm going with Jon tomorrow to fuel Surfeit."

The next morning Jon wasn't hard to find in the crowd. He was the only person with an armed guard. The two very conspicuous men stood against the bulkhead with a large, red, canister between them. As Justin approached, he noticed the biometric lock and the stickers warning of explosion and death. Without delay, the three men boarded the shuttle. The two friends spoke casually as they sat in the empty passenger section with the fuel canister between. The guard parked himself in the corner. Immediately the pilot departed for the short trip to Surfeit.

When they arrived, the guard remained on the transport. Jon took the fuel to the engine room. Justin headed to the bridge. Upon entering he was caught short. Mara was there talking to a technician. He had expected to find someone on the bridge, but Mara? "What are you... Oh," he said realizing she was holo projection.

Upon seeing Justin the tech turned to Mara and said, "It's been nice talking to you." He then turned to Justin, "You have the con."

He nodded and the man headed aft to the waiting shuttle.

"Did you spend the night hooked up in the cocoon?"

"No, Becca wouldn't let me, but we returned to the bridge early this morning. I think I scared that guy when I appeared here about an hour ago. I stayed, talked to him, and waited for you."

They continued the small talk as Justin began at one end of the bridge inspecting systems. Occasionally they would pause as he pulled a panel, slid under a workstation, or she needed to check something on the Exodus FTL drive. Almost an hour later, Justin was on his back examining the environmental backup system.

"I've got to go," Mara said. "I'm spinning up the FTL engines for the test hop."

"Good luck," he said with a grunt and slid deeper into the panel.

Moments later he heard Mara's voice came over the comm system, "Sound general quarters. Emergency FTL initialization."

"What?" Justin asked sliding out from under the workstation.

The computer voice of Surfeit declared, "Collision imminent."

Jon ran onto the bridge, "Did I hear...?" He stared at the holoview.

Still on the deck, Justin followed his gaze. Filling the screen was a bulging sensor eye painted with the symbol of the Nephilim.

## Chapter 24

Justin dashed to the captain's chair and strapped himself in.

Jon did the same at a nearby workstation. "Why haven't they shot at us?"

He silenced the collision alarm. "We're less than thirty meters from the dome. I imagine we look like a big blur on their sensors. They're probably wondering why they can't see anything off the bow."

"It won't take them long to figure it out and start shooting at Exodus—and us."

"Are we ready to jump?"

Jon shook his head. "I'd just started fueling the ship."

Looking down at the sensor console, Justin saw Titan ships blinking away and guns on the Nephilim ship attempting to lock on them. The Exodus, with Naomi and Mara on it, was still there. He knew Mara would be working frantically to jump the ship. "If we can't get away, maybe we can buy Exodus some time." Initializing the sub-light engines he said, "Let's ram this ship into the sensor array, okay?"

Jon took a slow, deep breath then nodded. He started to pull the seat harness tight then stopped. "I don't want to be captured."

Images of Titans burned at the stake flashed through Justin's mind. "No. I don't either." The engines roared to life. "I'll give it everything I've got."

Metal tore and screeched as Surfeit sliced through the thin dome, smashed the sensor dish, and continued through the hull below. The bridge contorted as Justin slammed into his harness.

Justin looked where Jon should have been. *He never tightened his harness.* Slowly his eyes swept forward along the ruined bridge. Crumpled at the forward end of the compartment he found Jon. Blood covered his face and much of his uniform. *He's dead.* He reached for the gun in the compartment beside the chair. "I won't be taken alive."

The image of a jump point formed in his mind as Mara, Naomi and a multitude of other Titans reached out to him and said, "Thank you."

Then Naomi's voice embraced him. *Be strong. I'll come for you.*

In his mind, Justin saw Exodus shoot across the event horizon and disappear.

A whoosh of air swept past. Darkness engulfed him.

\*  \*  \*

Justin struggled against the black shadows. He fought toward consciousness, aware on an instinctual level that he needed to wake up. Gradually he became aware that his eyes were open. Light and dark mixed with sound in a confusing montage.

A booming, insincere, voice proclaimed, "One of our guests awakes. Our party shall soon begin."

A murmur of excited voices reached Justin's ears as two blurs moved against the hazy background of his vision. He squinted and moved his head from side to side. Slowly one blur resolved into a man—a handsome man, about his age, with pink hair and wearing a purple and scarlet robe.

"How do you feel? Are you comfortable?"

A woman with blue hair stepped in his view. "You said he was scary. He doesn't look frightening. Handsome, yes, but not scary."

"He is very dangerous. Go sit down, dear. The feast will begin in a moment." He made a shooing motion.

The woman walked away in a huff as Justin looked about. He was lying on a couch in a large room. Behind the young man were about a dozen people dressed in wild colors and styles, reclining at couches arranged in a "U" shape before him. The clothing, make up, hair colors, and styles were so strange to him that it was hard to tell the men from the women. Both were more flamboyant than anything he had experienced. Beyond the colorful people the room extended into darkness.

Painfully Justin pushed himself to a seated position. It was then he noticed his clothing had been changed and he now wore a white robe. "Who are you?" he asked while checking the many scrapes and bruises about his torso and limbs.

"I am Remee, First Consul to Lord Enki, Nephilim of this ship."

Weeks ago, the thought of falling into the hands of the Titans caused him dread. Now his greatest wish was to be back with them as fear of what the Nephilim would do mushroomed within him.

He licked his parched lips with a dry tongue. "How long have I been unconscious?"

"About a standard day."

"Could I get some water?"

"Lord Enki has forbidden nourishment for both of you."

Three thoughts raced through Justin's mind. First, he was to be starved, probably before something worse was done to him. Next, he wondered where Jon was and lastly, could they get out of this place?

Slowly he looked over those in the room with him. None appeared to be soldiers or even armed. Most were young, about his age or a bit older, but they looked plump and pampered. Their bodies were soft with no tone to their muscles. *If I have to fight my way out of here it shouldn't be a problem.* As he scanned those around him with his eyes, he noticed Jon, also wearing a white robe and lying on the next couch to his left.

*Jon! Wake up!*

His eyelids shot open and without moving his head, he looked about. *Where are we?*

"Ah, our other guest has awakened. Let the celebration begin!"

*We're on the Nephilim temple ship.*

*Becca? Did the Exodus get away?*

"Yes." Justin sent the mental images of the jump to his friend's mind.

Jon smiled.

Servants entered and set tables before every guest, but not for the two prisoners.

*How did we get here? Why are we still alive? Jon asked.*

*I really thought you were dead. I'm not sure what happened, but I think the Surfeit bridge lost pressure. We passed out, but they got to us before we died.*

Jon rubbed his side carefully, and then winced.

*I'm sorry. I know we didn't want to be captured. I guess I failed.*

*Failed to kill us both?* Jon smiled. *I know you tried.*

The servants returned with dozens of plates, bowls and trays filled with, strange meat dishes, soups, fruits and salads of every description. Wines, and other drinks, in a wide variety of colors, were brought in. When the servants completed their task and departed, the tables were filled to overflowing.

Jon looked about. *I take it the food and drink are not for us.*

*I think we're going to have to fight them for it.*

Jon looked at others in the room and smiled. *Nice dinner they provided for us.*

"You two are talking with one another?" Remee twirled his fingers beside his head. "That famed Titan psychic ability. Am I right?"

Justin stared at him.

"We are not fools. We know what you are."

Justin remained silent.

Looking at both of them he said, "Do you deny it?"

Jon stayed still and mute, but Justin stood, stepped forward, and reached for a pitcher of water.

A blue flash lit the room accompanied by the sound of arcing electricity. Justin stumbled back and fell on the couch shaking his hand and cursing. He looked down where a blister had already formed.

Remee smiled. "Did I forget to mention the restraining field around each of you? I do apologize."

Justin started to reach out with his mind to strangle Remee, as he had Ferren, but realized it would accomplish little. He could kill Remee, but he would still be inside the restraining field.

Remee turned, "Bring on the musicians and dancers."

For what seemed like hours, the festivities continued. Justin and Jon were pointed at, stared at and talked about, but never addressed directly.

Someone clumsily spilled a drink on the table next to Jon. *I'd fight them all for a glass of water.*

Justin's stomach grumbled. *Or some food.* The field prevented them from getting to the food, but not the smells, or the satisfied thoughts of the dinners, from reaching them.

*What do you think they are doing?*

*Trying to weaken us with the smells and mental sensations from food and drink.*

*For what?*

Justin shrugged. *Perhaps for an interrogation.*

Several hours later Remee stepped to the center of the room and announced, "Our party must now conclude." Turning to Justin and Jon he said, "We bid you goodbye."

Within minutes the two were alone, able to talk to each other, but unable to leave. Justin was about to fall asleep when a voice boomed from everywhere.

"I am Enki, Lord of the Earth. I will speak with you now."

Jon shot to his feet, fists at the ready.

Justin rose and looked about.

Out of the darkness at the far end of the room emerged an old man in purple robes. He looked at them with haughty eyes.

Justin smirked in surprise. *This is the Nephilim.* Even as the thought crossed his mind, a cold breeze seemed to pass through him. He shivered and looked about, aware that other minds seemed to swim unseen in the air and linger close to the old man who called himself Enki.

"It has been many years since a Titan has stood before me." Enki smiled. "Now I have two." He walked past Justin, examining him like a trinket in the market. He stepped toward Jon, but paused and looked back at Justin. For a moment, a slight hint of confusion and concern crossed his face. Then he turned and proceeded to Jon.

"I have the power of life and death over you. You can die a slow lingering death within this restraining field or enjoy the favor of those who are willing to serve me."

*The spirit of the enemy fills this one. We cannot use him. Unless he renounces his faith.*

Stabbing at the ground he announced, "Kneel before your master and live."

Justin looked about the room. *Whose voices am I hearing?*

Jon looked at Justin. Fear filled his eyes. *The Prophet warns us about them. We're in the presence of fallen spirits. Beings that rebelled against God before the creation of the universe.* Jon's eyes swept the room. "I serve the God of the Prophet, not you."

In unison the voice declared. *Dispose of him.*

In a matter-of-fact voice Enki said, "Then you shall die."

Jon locked eyes with Justin. *Be strong.*

The floor seemed to turn to water under Jon and, like a rock, he disappeared into it.

## Chapter 25

Waves of pain from Jon surged over Justin's mind for a moment and then there was nothing. "What did you do to my friend?"

The unseen presence that clung close to Enki now dispersed around the room and declared with a thousand voices, *He is dead.*

Enki turned slowly toward him. "Your friend is dead."

Justin was shocked at the callous words from both the man and the voices that echoed from every corner of the room. Dread and sorrow filled him as he stumbled back onto the couch. His head slumped.

Justin looked up as Enki stepped closer.

The unseen voices declared, *We have fought this one long ago. How can it be? We watched him die.*

The young man watched as the old man's face turned from harsh to questioning.

A multitude of voices spoke, overlapped each other. *There are rules in this universe that even the foe must obey. Kill him. Kill him now!*

For just a moment alarm showed on Enki face.

*No!* A powerful new voice declared. *Recall that other time and place where we plotted to kill the Messenger. Remember how that was used against us. I shall not be tricked again. Make him hear what we propose.*

Enki stood before him, just beyond the restraining field. "Perhaps now you will listen to what we offer."

*Thirst.* The voices declared.

"Are you thirsty?" The old man retrieved a glass of water from the nearby table.

Justin's throat was parched, but he shook his head.

"Water is such a simple, easy gift to give." Enki drank the water slowly then tossed the glass aside. "I can give you water, but I offer you so much more. Anything you can imagine I can give you."

Justin smiled inwardly. *A ticket out of here.*

"I offer what most people only dream of. Do you know what that is?"

*Your defeat?* Justin shook his head again.

A thousand voices from around the room shouted in unison, *Power.*

"Power." Enki smiled. "I can give you that."

Dread, bordering on panic, filled Justin. All he wanted was to get away from Enki and the unseen voices, but he was sure that the offer of power did not include the power to leave.

"I offer you worlds. They are mine to give." Out of the darkness at the far end of the room came thousands of yellow, red, blue, and white points of light formed into a giant, floating, star map.

*These are our worlds. We are strong. We are legion.* A single thought came from the voices, *Choose a world. Worship us. Obey.*

"These are my worlds." Enki turned and walked toward the display. "My power grows stronger every day." Turning toward Justin he declared, "Choose what you desire and I will give it to you in return for your obedience and worship."

Justin slumped. He was hungry and desperate for water and his friend was dead. Silently he cursed the monster before him.

"Look at the worlds that could be yours. Which of these do you choose?"

Justin looked at Enki as an epiphany burst upon his mind. *What was that question again?*

The old man stared at him.

Justin smiled. *You can't hear my thoughts!*

A thousand voices demanded, *Answer us, human.*

"My patience is not endless. What is your answer?" Enki demanded.

Justin realized that while the audible voice came from Enki, he was merely a human puppet. The thoughts came from dark presence that he both felt and heard. However, neither the spirits nor the old wretch everyone called Nephilim could hear his thoughts.

Enki continued to speak, but Justin focused on the dark minds that floated about the room like ghosts. *I hear them, but I don't believe in ghosts.*

The Nephilim stepped closer. "If you will not agree to my terms, I can take your life just as I did your friend's but," the old man smiled, "I can take more than that from you."

The presence that had swirled around Enki passed effortlessly through the restraining field. Justin jumped to his feet as it enveloped him. He couldn't see it, but he felt like he was standing in a crowd. Many minds surrounded him. The demonic presence reached out and violated his every sense. Retched, rank and putrid it crawled into every pore of his body. Cold sweat covered him. No light illuminated the dark minds digging into his being. The bitter ache seeping into his bones reminded him of frigid Lepanto. His heart raced. The smell of death and decay permeated the air. He gagged. He tasted the rot as it leeched into his body.

*I don't believe in ghosts, but I do believe in evil.* As the malevolent presence burned into him he shouted, "God help me!"

The rancid spirits hurdled back.

As the world collapsed into darkness, Justin fell to the floor. When he awoke, sometime later, evil swirled around and over, but did not touch him.

Enki stepped closer. "Do you really believe in a god? Do you think he watches over you now?"

Justin ignored the questions. Through cracked lips he asked, "Why do you care?"

*He does not know the prophecy! He is a fool. How can he be so ignorant? His friends have abandoned him. He is ours to destroy. Kill him!*

"Fool! Are you so ignorant?" An ancient twisted face leapt from the darkness and stopped just short of his own. "How can you not know your own words?"

"What words?"

"The words of the prophecy." Enki walked along the edge of the restraining field. "Your friends and your god have abandoned you. Obey me and you shall have more than you ever dreamed."

Justin scowled at the ugly creature that stood before him. He now held a fledgling belief in the God of the Titans. He didn't know what he believed about demons, but he knew evil when he saw it and he rejected it now and forever. "No. Never."

"So be it."

Justin fell through the floor into darkness.

He landed on the metal floor with a bone-crushing thud and screamed in agony. His vision was blurred, but even in the darkness, he saw his abnormally twisted leg and the bone sticking out from it. Crying in pain, he pulled the useless leg from beneath him and tore the pant leg to fashion a makeshift tourniquet. The leg throbbed with each beat of his heart as it swelled to an abnormal size. He rested his head against the cold metal wall and tried not to look at the growing puddles of blood from a half dozen wounds of various magnitudes to his legs, chest and head.

Meager light entered the cell through a slit in the door. Justin couldn't see much, but what he could see was cold, gray, metal. Inches from him stood a simple bench and table fashioned from the same material as the walls and floor. If he had hit them on the way down he might be already dead. He was certain Jon had fallen into a similar dark dungeon.

His blood ran to a drain at the center of the cell. He tried to ignore the message of doom that it foreshadowed. He didn't regret crashing Surfeit into the sensor array. Naomi, Mara, Becca and thousands of others were safe because of it. *Do you agree Jon? Did we do the right thing?*

*There is no greater love…*

*Jon!*

*…than to lay down one's life for a friend.*

His mind reached out, but no answer came back. He shook his head. The mind that touched him was not Jon's. Perhaps it was just shock playing tricks on him.

As the minutes passed he slid from a sitting position into a less painful resting position on the floor. He felt little pain and knew that he was slipping deeper into shock. A weak smile spread across his face as Naomi and Mara came to mind. Weariness engulfed him and he closed his eyes.

Moments later, someone reached out and touched his thoughts. Perhaps it was a fellow prisoner, the one he sensed minutes ago. *Who are you, friend?*

Without a word, the unseen intellect washed over him, soothing him.

Justin pulled himself up and tightened the tourniquet. Mustering his mental faculties, he reached out to his unseen friend. *Thank you.*

Immediately Justin glimpsed a vast intelligence. He recalled stories of how several Titans had touched divinity. Justin's mind was like a raindrop rolling toward a vast sea. His thoughts focused on the intelligence just beyond his grasp. Desperately he wanted to be with it. He shifted his weight and pain shot through his leg, into his torso, like electric current.

Tears rolled down his face. *Are you really there? I don't want to die alone.*

*Before I formed you in your mother's womb, I knew you, and before you were born I set you apart.*

*Am I in shock or...can you be real?* He looked at the blood soaked band around his torn and twisted leg and the growing red pool. *I'm dying.*

*All flesh will die, but your time is not today.* A tiny spark floated above his feet. It grew stronger and brighter until the darkness of the cell had succumbed to the light. The luminous orb grew until Justin could feel its warmth on his skin and squinted, then closed his eyes. *Who are you?*

*I am the comforter. You must leave this place.*

He laughed. "I would if I could."

A deep rumble grew within the ship, silencing his sarcastic laugh. As it grew, the vessel shuddered and quaked until the heavy metal door to his cell sprang open.

Justin shot to his feet and stepped forward. Only then did he realize what he had done. Was it all a dream, the Comforter, the light? He touched the still-torn and blood-soaked pant leg. He took a step and then another without pain. *I'm healed.*

There was no time to sort it out. He released the tourniquet and ran from the cell.

## Chapter 26

Justin looked to his left, a dead end, and then right. The door at the end of the passageway was ajar. Another boom rocked the ship and the next cell creaked open. Fearing what he might see inside, he looked. "Jon?" His friend lay motionless on the floor. Pushing the door wide open, he entered the cell and pressed two fingers to Jon's neck. No pulse came back from the cool body. He cradled the head of his friend in his lap and with misty eyes bid him farewell.

Stepping into the passage he asked, "Why God? Why did I live and he die?" A thought came to mind as he ran down the passage. *Jon and I planned on dying when we rammed this ship. We both should be dead.*

From deep within came a calm assurance and a message more profound than words. *I spared both your lives for a purpose.*

*But, Jon is dead?*

*His purpose is complete. He showed you the way.*

*Way? Way of what?*

*Trust me.*

Justin reached the door as the guard attempted to lock it. Using his mind, he flung it wide open.

The man's pistol slid along the floor to the far side of the room. He stumbled as Justin's psychic fingers clasped tightly around his throat.

Dragging the guard along with his mind, Justin entered the room and noticed five doors. "Which way leads out of here?" He loosened the mental grip on the man's throat. "I only want my freedom. I won't hurt you."

The guard stammered, but the answer screamed from his mind.

Justin heard cries from the other cells. Had he been so consumed by his own problems that he hadn't heard their pleas or were they only now calling to him?

"Help me!" "Free me!" "Unlock the doors!"

It would at least create a distraction. Perhaps a few of them would find a way off the ship, and to freedom.

"Please, help us!"

Maybe they could help each other.

"Justin, is that you?"

Justin turned at the sound of a familiar voice.

"Ferren?"

The pirate smiled through the small window in the door. "Hello, old friend."

Justin turned back to the guard and was about to ask him how to open every cell, but that one.

"I forgive you for trying to kill me."

Justin laughed.

"Release me and we'll call it even."

He shook his head in disbelief.

"I know a way to get off this ship."

Justin knew the pompous pirate was playing him, but what if he did know a way off the ship? *I could read his mind? No, Ferren will fight it and it would take too much time.* Out of the darkness of the cell he could just discern the eyes of the pirate. *He must want off this ship as much as I do.* Turning to the guard Justin said, "Release the captives."

Still terrified, the man fumbled with the lever for a moment before he pulled it back.

Cell doors from all four-prison passageways clanged open. The central room filled with former captives.

One woman leapt at the guard, knocking him to the ground. Screaming accusations of abuse and torture she clawed and punched his face. Another woman fumbled with the pistol. Unable to get it to fire, she used it like a hammer on his face and skull.

Justin stepped forward to intervene, as others leapt upon the guard and beat him to a bloody pulp.

Standing beside Justin, Ferren smiled through yellow teeth. "Spunky girls."

Justin stared at him, then back at the motionless guard.

Ferren checked for a pulse and then shook his head. "Better do this while he's still-warm." The pirate grabbed the lifeless guard's wrist and dragged him to a rack containing two rifles. Placing the thumb on the biometric lock, he released the weapons. He kept one for himself and gave the other to Justin.

"Let's get out of here, old friend."

"We're not friends."

The pirate laughed as Justin headed for the door.

Ferren and the others caught up with him in the passageway.

The pirate tilted his head left. "This way." Approaching a dogged-down hatch he said, "I think the ship has gone to battle stations." Pointing to the levers holding the door tight he said, "We're going to have to open every one."

As Justin helped open it he asked, "Why did they lock you in a cell?"

"It's your fault. The buyers from Bristol turned out to be agents of Earth Empire. They wanted me to return with Naomi and they wanted information on anyone who might have assisted her." Ferren gave Justin a frustrated glance. "It turned out you were assisting her, you were a Titan, and both of you fled together. They made it quite clear that I must return quickly with both of you."

They stepped through the open hatch into a large storage bay.

Justin gave a wry smile. "I knew you were following me…."

"But I didn't get you. The imperial navy hunted me down, boarded my ship, killed my crew, and captured me." He shook his head. "You've really messed up my life."

"Messed up your life? You tried to kidnap Naomi and Mara and I think you would have killed me to do it."

Together they reached the next hatch. Ferren smiled, "How is your sister?"

*Fine now that she's safe from you and the Empire.* Justin walked away, letting Ferren, and others, work on the hatch ahead. Scanning the ragtag group of former prisoners, Justin estimated they numbered about forty. He noticed the woman that had used the guard's pistol as a hammer. Walking up to her he asked, "Do you know how to use the weapon?" Since she had tried unsuccessfully to shoot the guard before beating him with it, he was certain the answer was, "No."

With a shake of the head, she confirmed it.

As they walked down the passageway to toward the next hatch, he showed her how to release the safety and turn on the targeting mechanism.

Almost at a whisper she said, "I saw you do things. People are whispering. Are you a…" Her voice trailed off.

"A Titan? Yes."

"They taught us that all the Titans were killed in the years after the Battle for Earth, that you were all evil monsters."

"They lied."

She nodded. "About a lot of things."

Tearing a rag from his torn trouser leg, he wiped the gun clean of the guard's blood and returned it to her. "What's your name?"

"Prisca," she replied staring at the weapon.

"I'm Justin."

Several people worked to open the hatch just ahead. Ferren had gradually moved toward the back of the group and was now just a meter away. Justin turned to the pirate, "Where are we going?"

"To the cargo bay. That's where they have my vessel."

Justin started to object, but reconsidered. If the temple ship was at battle stations, no one should be in the cargo bay.

Another boom seemed to confirm the pirate's thinking that they were in a battle. He shook his head wondering what the chances were of flying a ship to freedom in the midst of combat.

As the pirate stepped through the hatch he asked, "Are they fighting your people?"

He was about to say he didn't know when he realized he could find the answer. Slowly Justin opened his mind. He sensed marines and sailors nearby, but none approaching their location. Gradually he widened his mental search until his mind touched someone familiar. *Naomi?*

*Justin? Where are you?*

He did his best to tell her as they opened the next hatch. *We're headed toward the cargo bay.*

*Is Jon with you?*

*No. The Nephilim killed him. I'm with Ferren and some other prisoners.*

She cursed both the Nephilim and the pirate. *Kill Ferren when you get to the cargo bay.*

Justin ignored her anger. *Where are you?*

*Onboard the temple ship with a company of shadow warriors. Fighters from a nearby carrier have damaged the vessel's engines so they shouldn't be going anywhere until we can retrieve you.*

"Yes," Justin said.

Ferren, working on another hatch, looked puzzled. "Yes? Yes what?"

"Yes, this ship is fighting Titans."

Guarded glances led to an agitated murmur amongst the former prisoners.

The pirate shook his head. *Great, stuck between the Nephilim and the Titans. What do I do?*

Justin smiled as he easily read Ferren's thoughts and vowed to keep a close eye on him. Turning toward the crowd in the passageway he called out, "Listen to me. The Nephilim who imprisoned you lied. Yes, I am a Titan, but you are now free. If you wish to leave, do so. However, other Titans are fighting to reach me and, if you are with me, they will help you." His eyes moved from face to face. Only Prisca's appeared calm. "We need to move quickly toward the cargo bay." Fear and confusion still etched their faces, but they followed.

Dread from imperial marines washed over Justin as they approached the next hatch. When they opened it, he heard the rapid blast and ping of gunfire. *Naomi, if other Titans are onboard, why am I only sensing you?*

*We do not want the Nephilim to gain information from our thoughts.*

*They can't read them.*

*Are you sure?*

*I read Enki's mind and I heard the voices of the things, spirits…whatever, that controlled him, but they could not hear my thoughts.* Justin projected the memory of his epiphany to Naomi.

She laughed in delight. *That is why the Nephilim kept their distance from me. They didn't want me to know their powers were limited.* Again, she laughed and passed on the news.

Waves of fear, fright and terror came to Justin from every direction. Many Titan soldiers were afraid, but the imperial troops were near panic. As Titan units telepathically reported their exact positions, naval units increased fire. Booms reverberated as the ship shuddered.

In addition to the fighter carrier, Naomi advised him that two Titan battleships were off the bow in the blind spot he had created. *We have a troop transport in a launch bay we captured, but we cannot carry all of you. I hate to admit it, but Ferren has a good idea. Get to the cargo bay. We'll block the imperial troops from the area.*

In a loud whisper, Ferren called ahead to Prisca, telling her to turn right at the next junction. "We're almost there."

As Prisca did so, shots rang out and she threw herself back around the corner and against the bulkhead. The man behind her froze at the edge of the passageway then fell to the ground, as more shots were fired.

Justin stepped around the wide-eyed Prisca to the corner. The dead man was at his feet. He peered down the passageway and saw only two marines firing from the wide hatch that was the entrance to the cargo bay.

Naomi reached out to him. *We are coming from the aft, but we have engaged at least a company of marines and they are not retreating or surrendering. She paused. We are going to have to kill them all.*

*We're at the forward door. There's only two marines. We'll be in the bay shortly.*

Leaning up against the bulkhead, Justin turned to the others. "I have a plan. I'll fire then run for the other side of the passageway. As I do," he pointed to Ferren and Prisca, "both of you shoot." He looked at the woman. "Okay?"

She nodded.

Justin took a deep breath and projected his thoughts toward the marines. *Look high.* He thrust the point of his rifle around the corner at shoulder height and fired a single shot, then immediately dropped to a crouch. As shots pinged high above him he fired low at the marines and raced for the far wall.

Ferren hesitated.

Prisca stepped into the open and fired two shots. One marine fell and the other ran. "Come on," she shouted as she ran down the passage.

Justin shook his head. *That was too easy.* "Prisca. Wait." She paused and together, with Ferren, they approached the cargo doors. At the entrance, he explained to them what Naomi had told him about the fight just aft. "Why are we meeting light resistance and they are fighting soldiers to the death?"

"Just be thankful, friend." Ferren waved the others forward. "Come on let's get to my ship."

## Chapter 27

Emergency lights revealed the line of transport ships that stood thirty meters from them. Cargo bins were stacked beside many of the vessels creating a partial wall down the middle of the bay.

Ferren pointed forward. At the head of the line, ten ships forward and closest to the launch bay doors, Justin spotted the Acheron, Ferren's ship. He looked about. Although he could sense the presence of hundreds of Titans, and even more Norms, the vast place appeared empty.

As Ferren hurried toward his vessel, Justin stifled a chuckle. The fat pirate's gait was more like a pregnant waddle than a run. Two meters behind the brigand, Justin was more cautious as he continued along the bulkhead of the dark, cavernous, compartment. Looking over his shoulder, he signaled Prisca.

Still clutching the pistol, she crept forward. The other prisoners all but surrounded her, apparently finding comfort in either her or the pistol she held.

Justin moved cautiously ahead. Emotions ranging from apprehension to outright terror deluged him. He followed the pirate at a guarded pace, looking left and right. Intuition shouted caution. Could it merely be the frightened people around him? There were so many, so near. He shook his head. *So near.* He stopped and stared at the line of cargo bins and ships. No, something was very wrong.

Light filled the compartment.

Armed imperial troops poured from several transports and appeared atop nearby cargo bins. Justin stiffened and the others froze. Within seconds, a company of marines surrounded him and the other captives.

A major stepped forward. "Lay down your weapons."

Justin's eyes remained on the troops before him, until he heard a rifle drop onto the metal deck. Looking left, he saw Ferren, twenty meters away, with marines on either side.

The officer repeated his command.

With his eyes fixed on the major, Justin slowly and deliberately placed his gun on the ground. The major then order them to kick the weapons toward him. Justin and Ferren complied.

The line of marines behind the major parted. Even before he could see Enki, Justin knew the Nephilim was approaching because the demonic voices preceded him.

*We are legion. We are strong. We are victorious.*

Through the opening in the line of marines Enki stepped forward, followed by Remee. A smug smile grew on Enki's face as their eyes met.

*Your plan failed. We have killed you once before! We have defeated you again.*

Justin knew the real thought and power came not from the man before him, but from the unseen voices he was hearing. He wondered how the demons knew him and why they hated him.

"Great Enki," Ferren proclaimed in a proud voice as he walked toward Justin, "as I promised, I have brought you this Titan."

Enki and Remee looked at him incredulously.

Justin didn't bother to even look at Ferren. He never expected anything else. The pirate had been true to his nature.

Something hard touched Justin's back and he glanced over his shoulder. The other captives were closely behind him now, but Prisca stood right behind him.

*Can you hear me? I still have the pistol.*

Prisca's thoughts came through clearly to Justin. He gave a slight nod, but wondered how the one weapon might help.

*You hid your presence from us in the cell, but we watched in the passageways. We knew your plan.*

Justin tried to block out the unseen voices.

The ship shuddered with another explosion, but Enki casually smiled. "Did you think I would not watch the passageways of my own temple?"

*The Enemy has established rules in this universe. You should not be here. We killed you centuries ago.*

A soldier ran up to the Major and Remee. Justin couldn't hear his words, but he could read his thoughts. The Titans were seconds away from entering the cargo bay.

Enki nodded as Remee passed the message. "Such a shame, I was hoping to play with him for a while and then kill him."

"Even if you kill me, you've lost." Justin exclaimed. "The Titans will destroy this ship and you along with it."

*When we kill you, we change this future. You will never become the prophet to the Titans.*

"You are such a fool," Enki said with a shake of his head. "How do you become the prophet of the Titans?"

Those words from both the demons and the Nephilim shocked Justin. The prophet died centuries ago. *How can they think I am the prophet?*

With a dismissive toss of the hand Enki signaled the major, "Kill him."

Justin felt the officer's hesitation and even his fear that a firing squad might hit civilians, but all he said was, "Yes, my lord." The major called three soldiers forward. Except for Prisca, all the former prisoners moved as far away from Justin as the marines would allow.

*Naomi, now would be a good time to arrive.*

"Ready."

Justin looked over his shoulder to tell Prisca to move away when he sensed her intent.

"Aim."

"No!" Justin shouted as Prisca ran forward firing wildly. One of the three executioners fell. Blood streamed from his chest. The startled soldiers returned fire, hitting Prisca repeatedly.

The lights blinked and then darkness filled the bay.

The Major shouted for his men to cease-fire as the emergency lights came on.

Justin knelt beside Prisca's bloody body. Rage filled his mind. He lifted his eyes from her lifeless body to Enki and the two remaining soldiers beside him. With a brush of his arm, he threw the two soldiers into air. They landed with a thud upon the marines behind them. He then focused his mind on Enki, wrapping the force of his thoughts around the Nephilim's throat and preventing him from speaking and breathing.

Enki's arms flailed and pointed at Justin.

Remee, his eyes darting between the suffocating Enki and the soldiers, pointed at Justin and the other captives. "All of them…kill…shoot…do something."

A deep, angry, growl filled the cargo bay. The soldiers continued to point their weapons at Justin, but their heads looked in all directions as the growl grew in intensity. Soldiers standing atop the bins went into a panic of wild shots and shouts as dogs leapt upon them.

The Titan Canine Corps had arrived.

Justin sensed the presence of Thor, the dog that had befriended him that first day aboard Exodus. Images of the

Canine Corps, rushing single file along the air ducts to the cargo bay, filled his mind. *Good Thor.*

The soldiers below shifted their aim to the top of the containers, but only terrified soldiers at the edge of the bins were visible.

An explosion reverberated from the rear of the cargo bay. Darkness grew as gunfire shattered several emergency lights.

Imperial marines paid little attention to Justin as they rushed past and engaged oncoming Titan forces.

Justin's eyes shot back to where Enki should have been. He was gone and so was Ferren. Several former captives were dead on the deck, but others used what cover was available as they headed toward the Acheron. Seeing no fighting at that end of the bay, Justin picked up the pistol Prisca had used and, staying low, headed in that direction.

*Justin what is your location?* It was Leonidas' voice in his head.

Are you okay? Naomi asked.

He did his best to answer both as he took cover.

*Get out of there quick,* Naomi commanded. *Most of the imperial marines are in that area.*

*Yes, thank you, I do know that.* Retreating marines set up a position near Justin. He sent them a mental misdirection, *enemy on the left,* then darted to the right behind a bin. Turning his attention back to Naomi he said, *I am trying not to draw attention to myself so I won't get killed.* Running to the far corner, he glanced around. *But, with all this gunfire that is going to be hard.* Behind the next cargo bay, he saw Thor and two other dogs.

*Come.*

Justin obeyed and dove toward Thor, sliding to a stop at his front paws. Looking up he smiled.

The dog licked his face, turned, and trotted off.

From about six meters away, Thor looked back. *Come.*

Justin rose and followed the dogs as they climbed up the cargo bins. Ramps and strategically placed crates had allowed workers to climb the bins. Where these were not available, the dogs were adept at jumping.

After a couple of jumps Justin, bruised and hot, started moving crates.

Once they reached the top, a canine squad greeted him with nudges and nuzzles. Crawling to the edge of a bin with several dogs, he looked down on a sweeping vista of the battle. The imperial marines held a jagged and uneven line between him and the oncoming Titans. From his vantage point, he could see the plan of battle clearly. The Titans were in an arc largely along the line of the cargo bins. Their front line kept enough pressure on the Earth forces to keep them pinned down, while most Titan units pushed slowly forward behind the cargo bins and transports. Many of the imperial soldiers were firing into shadows where, Justin was certain, no Titans were. He became convinced they were being misdirected, similar to the way he had soldiers look one way as he went the other. However, the only ground that the imperial marines surrendered was paid for with blood.

As Justin watched, he understood why the Nephilim were so intent on destroying his kind. The Titans had started out as the best and brightest humans and with work and training had melded into a well-disciplined army. However, over the years, the Titans had changed, becoming more with both psychic abilities that allowed them to know the true intent of those around them, and a faith in something greater than the earthly government that originally sent them. Justin knew that Titans would never be pawns of the Nephilim.

The dogs growled and, all but Thor, headed down toward the deck.

Gunfire immediately below his position grabbed Justin's attention. *Naomi where are you?*

"Here," she said with a gasp.

Justin turned at the sound of her voice.

She smiled and knelt down near him. "Your mind has been wide open for a while. I have been following you."

Sliding away from the edge so he could kneel beside her, he grinned. "I'm glad you reached me. Now let's get out of here."

An explosion thundered through the bay. Alarms sounded over the battle. "Decompression Warning. Evacuate the main cargo bay."

Almost immediately, Justin felt a breeze as the compartment began losing atmosphere, but a new and horrible feeling swept over him. The blast had struck Leonidas.

Justin fell to his knees.

Naomi opened her mind to Justin and thereby to Leonidas. She wrapped her arms around Justin and with her mind comforted them both.

As the life flowed from Leonidas, Justin shared his jail cell encounter with God. *You will be with him soon. You will see your family again.*

The mind of Leonidas faded and then was gone.

Justin turned to Naomi "You shouldn't have come here. It's too dangerous. You could be killed."

"I don't think so, my destiny is with you."

Justin thought that a romantic notion and a bit out of place in the midst of battle, but the words silenced his objections. "The Acheron isn't far," he said, "let's go."

As they moved away from the battlefield, Naomi updated the Titan second-in-command.

*The atmospheric pressure is dropping fast, the commander reported. We have to retreat. Get to the Acheron and launch. Our fighters will cover you.*

There were few marines at that end of the compartment and they were either moving away from them, misdirected or quickly dispatched by Thor, Naomi and Justin.

The air was cold and moist as they arrived at the Acheron and the breeze had become a steady wind. Both the cargo and passenger hatches of the pirate ship were closed and locked. Together they moved along the belly of the ship to a small maintenance hatch. This they found unlocked. Once Naomi was in the hatch, Justin handed Thor up to her. Thor insisted upon leading the way down a narrow maintenance tube to one of the engineering compartments.

Once they were out of the tube Justin suggested, "Let's get to the bridge and see if we can activate the sensors and weapons."

Thor led the way along the main passageway.

As the three of them entered the bridge, Thor growled.

From the captain's chair, Ferren smiled. "Welcome aboard old friend."

## Chapter 28

Naomi aimed her rifle at Ferren's head, while Thor inched forwarded, growling.

The pirate continued to grin. "I've got the reactor and sensors online. The engines will take more time. Unfortunately, they've unloaded the missile bays and discharged the lasers and particle beam weapons."

"Perhaps they don't trust you," Naomi snarled.

Ferren shrugged, but Justin sensed his fear.

The growing storm, visible on the view screen, captured Justin's attention. Tools and other small objects were already flying in the wind. As it continued, the danger to the Acheron would grow as even the large cargo bins creaked and scraped their way closer to the hole in the hull. Something either flying or scraping along would hit Acheron in a vital location. Justin knew they needed to leave quickly and would need Ferren. "There will be no more killing, for now. We need to get out of the cargo bay."

Justin switched the view forward to the bay doors. "Can you open them?"

The pirate shook his head. "I can't access the system. Even if I did, it requires a code that I don't have. What about you? Can't you open them?"

The day Justin killed Garrett flashed through his mind. He saw again the way he had fixed his eyes on the bay doors and imagined opening them, the old lock cracked and split with a pop. The door shrieked and blew away. "I'll try to open them. I've done it before." Using the screen image, he reached out with his mind searching for the door. There would be something, some flaw to exploit or some latch that could be moved to release the doors. Many things flashed through his brain: circuits, panels, metal, but it was unfocused and fleeting. "I need to see it with my own eyes."

"No." Naomi said. "It is already dangerous outside. If you blow the hatch you will be sucked out and…."

"An emergency shield *should* activate," Ferren said casually.

Naomi's face went stone cold. "We knocked out power to the bay as we fought our way in,"

"There *should* be an emergency back up," Ferren rebutted.

Her face turned progressively deeper shades of red. "How long would that hold?"

"Probably long enough," Ferren said.

Justin felt strangely calm about his decision. "I'm going out. If somehow I am the prophet, or will be, I'll be okay. If I'm not the prophet, it's best that everyone know that now." He stepped toward the hatch.

Naomi reached out to him. "I know you will be okay, but I am still afraid."

"So am I, but I can do this…"

She held his hand tight.

"…but the longer I wait the more dangerous this becomes."

She released his hand.

Reaching the airlock, Justin looked out the portal hoping to see at least part of the bay doors. He couldn't. Reluctantly he opened the airlock to the storm. The wind hit him like a punch to the face. He grabbed the steel handhold as he stepped outside and looked forward. He could see the bay doors. *Focus. Focus.* Nothing came back to his mind. He yelled into the wind. "God, do you want me to do this? Help me!" Slowly the circuits that locked the doors formed in his mind. *One little spark. That is all I....*

The doors budged. The wind shifted. Thrown forward against the hull, Justin barely kept his grip on the handle. Red lights flashed and alarms sounded above the storm. A translucent shield appeared as the doors inched open. The wind shifted again and Justin was thrown into the airlock. "Thank you, God," he said getting to his feet.

The holographic image of a swirling vortex greeted Justin as he stepped back on the bridge. "You got the engines online?"

"No," the pirate said staring at the approaching wormhole. "I launched using thrusters and then Imperium attempted to jump."

"Attempted?"

Naomi tapped the side of her head. "Our people are saying the temple ship engines are out of control. The wormhole is distorting space-time."

"We should get out of here," Justin said.

Ferren nodded. "If the engines were running, believe me I would. We're being pulled into the temple ship vortex."

Justin watched with growing apprehension. "Can anyone reach us in...?"

"Time?" The pirate shook his head. "No." The pirate reached into a compartment beside the captain's chair and pulled out a flask. "Care for a drink, old friend?"

Justin shook his head.

The pirate took one long drink and then another.

Justin stepped close to Naomi and embraced her. "You shouldn't have come to me."

Naomi smiled. "My destiny is with you." She kissed him gently.

Thor nudged his way between them.

Justin's petted the dog and then shifted his gaze to the approaching event horizon. "You said earlier that your destiny was with me." He looked at Naomi. "What did you mean?"

"Remember that day on the bridge when you and I did the drawings of Earth Empire warships?"

Justin nodded and sat at one of the bridge stations.

"I said I found things that convinced me the Titans were telling the truth."

"Yes," Justin recalled. "You were doing research in the central archive and needed more time to finish."

"I finished. The information is all on the slate Becca loaned to me."

"What did you find?"

She reached out and took his hand. "I found me…and you…together."

Thor rested his head on Justin's lap and seemed to smile.

The Acheron shuddered, crossed the event horizon, and disappeared.

\* \* \*

Mara didn't knock as she entered carrying a large box.

Becca hardly looked up from the couch where she sat with her newborn baby across her lap. Since the battle, she and Becca had shared quarters.

Mara pulled a slate from the box and handed it to Becca. "I think this is the one you loaned to Naomi."

Lying on a pillow in the corner of the room, one of Thor's puppies raised its head.

Becca sat the slate on the table beside her.

The black puppy raced across the room and disappeared into the next.

Becca's eyes dropped to the sleeping baby. *I'll never see your father again and you'll never know him. Why did he have to die? Over a hundred Titans dead and thousands on the temple ship. Why did any of them have to die. Why?* She took a deep breath and let it out it in ragged spasms. *Why God? Why did Jon die?*

As Mara continued to unpack the box, the last puppies that Thor sired ran into the room and formed a semi-circle around the table with the slate. Their heads tilted toward the tabletop as they jostled around it.

"Go away," Becca commanded.

The puppies crowded around the table like there was food on top, but there was only the slate. Becca reached for it when one of the puppies jumped up and rested both paws on the edge of the device. The pup cocked his head to the side, locked eyes with Mara, and touched the screen with its front paw.

A holographic image of Naomi appeared. "Originally, I set out to find the truth about the Alien and Titanomachy wars. Jon suggested that I research the history of the Prophet. I did and discovered my future, or is it my past." She smiled, but there was sadness in her voice.

Mara joined Becca on the couch as Naomi continued.

"There are few surviving images of Justin the Prophet and what remains are locked away. The Prophet's book warns, I have been told, to worship only the creator, never the creation, and especially never him. So, these few remaining images of the Prophet are only seen when needed for research. Jon encouraged me to do the research and Olham, keeper of the archive, allowed me access."

An image of Justin, Mara's brother, formed in the air. Several others stood in the background around him.

"This is the oldest image of the Prophet."

Becca gasped. Mara leaned forward.

Naomi continued. "The woman in the background is identified only as his wife."

Mara reached out as if to touch the people in the image. It was then that Becca realized the woman in the back was Naomi. Other images formed in the air including a few drawings of both him and Naomi.

"These fragile sketches are the work of the Prophet. It is clear to me now," Naomi continued, "that Justin and I will journey back in time to the end of the Alien War. I don't understand how, but he will come to faith in God and through him all Titans will come to believe. The Justin we know will become the Prophet. His life will be difficult and his death will be gruesome, but I love him and willingly I will follow him."

Made in the USA
Charleston, SC
09 July 2013